THE HUNTING-GROUND

An Irish photographer in the West Indies inadvertently becomes involved in a mysterious plane crash of which he is the sole apparent witness, and with more than just snaps of humming-birds in his camera.

'Exquisitely calculated to provide a quietly understated but breathlessly urgent thriller.'
New York Times

The Hunting-Ground

Francis Clifford

CORONET BOOKS
Hodder Paperbacks Ltd., London

_To the best of the author's knowledge the island
depicted in this story does not exist. All the characters
are equally imaginary_

Printed and bound in Great Britain for Coronet Books,
Hodder Paperbacks Ltd, St Paul's House, Warwick Lane,
London EC4P 4AH by Cox & Wyman Ltd, London, Reading
and Fakenham

ISBN 0 340 15145 5

A man who goes out to meet trouble will have a short walk.

Johann Georg Zimmermann

WALK – *n*, the action, or an act, of walking ... a perambulation in procession: a walking-race: gait: that in or through which one walks ... a path or place for walking ... distance as measured by the time taken to walk it: conduct: course of life, sphere of action ... a hunting-ground.

Chambers's Twentieth Century Dictionary

For
MARK

CHAPTER ONE

THE humming-bird nests were in a concentration of juniper shrubs on the hillside and Brennan spent all of four uncomfortable hours getting his pictures. The nearest and most exposed of the nests was about seventy-five feet diagonally below him. There were two young Copper-rumps in it, newly hatched, sightless and naked, as ugly as the tiny parent birds were exquisite. When the female hovered above the nest, time and again the quivering miracle of its suspended flight almost made Brennan forget what he was about. He was using a Retina reflex with 150-mm telephoto attachment and an ultra-violet filter, but as always with humming-birds his main problem was shutter-speed. Poised, their blurred wing-beats were in excess of fifty to the second, and when they resumed normal flight they suddenly became an iridescent flash that practically defeated the eye.

By six o'clock he had exhausted his stock of colour-film. The sun was beginning to plunge into the hills and the light was thickening fast. His intention had been to descend to the road well before nightfall, but the longer he stayed and the more cramped he became the harder it was to drag himself away. It was days since he had been so well rewarded. He reloaded with black and white and patiently experimented with that until it was pointless to go on. All around him the forest sang and whispered. Bats were already sketching swift patterns across scarlet banks of cumulus in the west and the tree-frogs had started to zing. At length Brennan eased himself clear of the protruding ledge of moss-skinned rock on which he had sweated for most of the afternoon. Bleary, gratified, aching, he stood up and stretched. One hundred and twenty worthwhile shots—no one could have wished for more. And there had been some good ones, too; pretty wonderful, a few of them, he felt sure.

It was too late to start down now. The Land-Rover was fifteen hundred feet below, cached close to the road, and it would take him at least an hour to reach it—three-quarters of which time he would be risking his neck. There was no track and in places the slopes were precipitous. It wasn't the first occasion that single-mindedness had caused him to spend the night out of doors, and it wouldn't be the last. He gathered his gear together philosophically, packed the worn pigskin holdall, then moved to a less precarious spot. The Caribbean dusk was coming down like a velvet curtain. There was some beer in the pocket of the holdall, which he drank direct from the can. Between warm gulps of it he finished what was left of his jaded-looking food-pack. Then he lit a cigarette and watched the purple dark close quickly in; the vast stars prick through.

He had stranded himself in far more disagreeable places. The scratching of the forest did not alarm him and there would be no rain. A little stiffness in the morning was a small price to pay for such a profitable session. He lay on his back and drew on the cigarette, content, picturing the humming-birds in his mind's eye—the Bee humming-bird in particular, with its bright ruby crown and ear tufts, two inches long from bill to tail, hovering fantastically inside the trumpet of a yellow hibiscus on the slopes below. He had been lucky and captured that, too : f8, 1000th of a second . . . All in all it had been quite a day.

Only when he thought about Alison did he regret not having quit earlier. And, with a touch of jealousy that surprised him, he found himself wondering whether Frank Merchant had been over to the Oasis Club during the late afternoon for more of her coaching. For someone who claimed to be a novice Merchant played as good an all-round game as almost anyone who came to the Oasis, and the supposed weakness of his back-hand was beginning to look like an excuse to get Alison to himself on the practice-court. Just a blasted excuse . . .

The sound of the plane reached into Brennan's oblivion like a drill, boring deeper and deeper until it shook him into consciousness. For a leaden moment or two he couldn't remember where he was, or why : nor could he grasp what caused the din. He blinked sluggishly at the sky, scattered wits imagining a storm. A million stars denied the possibility but the roar intensified, shot through with a demented high-pitched whine.

Brennan had an uncanny sensation, as if time were being momentarily held in check. He jerked on to his elbows, gaping up, and as he did so the plane flashed directly overhead. It was enormous, so low that it seemed almost to scrape the top of the cedar under which he lay. The air shuddered and the thunder of the jets deafened him, jarring through the bone of his skull.

"Jesus, Mary and Jo—"

It had gone from view before he gained his feet, gone fast, the wings dark and glinting, the windows along the fuselage ablaze with light. For perhaps a couple of seconds he stood quite still, rooted in an intolerable tension that was part dread, part disbelief. Then he heard the first snapping noise. It was absolutely distinct from the engine's fury, brittle, for all the world like teeth crunching into a stick of celery. Almost immediately the noise was repeated, separated from the first by the minutest fraction of time. He didn't need to guess what it meant. Soon there was a machine-gun burst of impacts by the score and he knew that the plane had started to plough into the forest roof. But whether he began to move before or after the final crescendo of the crash he was never able to recall. All he was sure about was the way in which the rim of the hillside was flash-bulbed into violet brightness and the brief yet terrifying silence that held sway until the birds began their startled screaming.

As he blundered upwards he was guided by glimpses of a flickering orange glow; but this didn't last. Starlight gave ghostly shape to his surroundings and he thrashed his way through evergreen thickets and tangles of hanging lianas with the desperation of someone pursued. Habit had made him grab his holdall and the slung weight of it frequently threw him off balance. He kept on for as long as he could without pausing, but eventually he was forced to stop. He peered at his watch, as if by establishing the time he could link what had happened to reality and rid himself of disbelief. It was a quarter to six. Lungs burning, sweat pouring in greasy streams, he stared wildly about him. The echoing bursts of bird-song had lost their shrill alarm but his own sense of shock hadn't flagged. Inaction seemed a crime and within seconds he again began to stumble in what he believed was the right direction, traversing the hillside as he climbed.

A shadowless pre-dawn light presently came to his aid. Soon he was able to pick some sort of route and spare himself the worst hazards. Even so, in half an hour he couldn't have covered more than half a mile. Colour was beginning to tinge the cavernous vault of the forest and pale patches of sky showed through the froth of the tallest trees. He paused again, searching for the first tell-tale signs of disaster while the ground seemed to sway from side to side and a mosquito-like buzzing filled his ears. It was impossible to say how long had elapsed between his fleeting sight of the plane and the sound of its death. But reason told him that he must by now be close to where it had struck and his imagination was increasingly at work, testing him with visions of what he might find.

The first definite clue came when he neared the crest of the ridge. Then—a little below him and some distance to his left—he noticed that the top of a huge rosewood had been splintered off. He struggled down towards its base and chose a fresh line to follow. It was at least a hundred yards before he saw anything else significant—a section of wing lodged high in some shattered branches, complete with engine-pod. From there on only a blind man could have lost his way. A tangled cul-de-sac had been scythed along the forest's sloping floor. A thin stream of smoke obscured the far end, but at Brennan's point of entry the aftermath of the plane's passage was nakedly exposed—deformed scraps of metal, scored earth, flattened undergrowth, uprooted and fractured stumps of trees.

The silence was eerie. The white, ripped-off tail stood on its own to one side of the swath, wrapped around with creepers. He ignored it and ran on. Here and there he began to pass disgorged contents of the fuselage—a cushion, plastic trays, an old-fashioned suit-case, towels . . . Whatever hope impelled him towards the crumpled mainplane had shrivelled to nothing well before he reached it. No one could have survived this. He remembered the violent flash and the curdled flames that followed. The fire hadn't lasted, but it had burned savagely. Now there was blackened metal and a hot stench that caused him to back away with a stomach-squirm of revulsion. He shook his head, as a dog shakes water from its coat, and tried to spit out the taste.

"God above," he whispered hoarsely. "How many?"

A crack-crack of heat answered him: sparks flew in an eruption of grey dust. Both wings had gone and the nose had dug in deep. The gaping end of the fuselage was tilted sharply into the air and he was almost thankful that he couldn't see inside or get close enough to squint through the windows. He moved clear and gazed along the corridor the plane had made. It looked as if it had been shelled. Litter was everywhere—large and small; someone's hat, a wheel from the undercarriage, its tyre shredded to ribbons, more galley utensils, an incongruous length of dark red curtain attached to a chrome rail . . . With heightened awareness he noted all he saw—in particular the way in which the timber had been sliced through at different levels, the raw stumps rising in rough gradation away from him.

He walked towards the tailplane, the sense of urgency supplanted by a dreadful feeling of impotence. All around the tail the scrub was flattened and torn up, as if an animal had lashed from side to side in its death throes. There were slight signs of scorching; more spewed-out debris. About ten yards away he came across the body of a man. At first sight it looked as if he had tripped and gone sprawling; scarcely more than that. But when Brennan went to turn him over he was confronted by a face so hideously lacerated that it made him recoil. Even now he wasn't prepared for such nauseating proof that he was wasting his time. Soon there was another body, dark-suited like the other, but broken in such a way that it wasn't necessary even to touch him to provoke Brennan's unconscious gesture of futility.

The sun was pushing long level rays through the surrounding trees. A gaudy butterfly jazzed past, advertising life. His thoughts were going all ways at once. Who were they? Now the questions were beginning, demanding explanations for mutilation and sudden death. What went wrong? . . . An extra hundred feet or so and the plane would have cleared the ridge. He made another tour of the stricken area, but found nothing to justify his remaining there. The only practical course open to him was to descend to Pozoblanco as soon as he could: without guidance a search-party might blunder about for hours on end. He returned to the vicinity of the tailplane and covered the two bodies, one with some cushions, the other with a travelling-rug. Ants had found the blood already and he didn't doubt that the flies would be there by the time he returned, but it seemed the least he could do.

And then, as he straightened, he saw the figure of a man lodged in a near-by silk-cotton tree. The discovery was unnerving and his skin crawled. The man was about twenty feet up and Brennan's first impression was that he was alive; watching him. For a deranged moment or two he imagined that he must have climbed there and in a release of nervous tension he spoke to him. Incredibly, what he said was: "Are you all right?"—though before the words were out he knew there would be no answer.

Even more incredible was the fact that the man was sitting in a seat with the safety-belt still secured round his waist. Brennan moved closer, unable to believe his eyes. There were no visible marks of violence; no expression of split-second horror. The podgy, zinc-grey face looked utterly peaceful and the hands were slack across the thighs. Only the absence of a shoe on one of the dangling feet, and the angle at which the foot was turned in towards the other, hinted at the force that must have blasted him clear, seat and all, as the plane broke in two.

Brennan's first thought was to get him down, but there was no way of reaching him. The thick, smooth trunk offered no holds and the lowermost branches were too high. A ladder was needed; ropes. In any case, where was the urgency? He was as dead as the others, more freakishly, his resting-place more bizarre, but just as dead.

Instinctively, Brennan drew his camera from the holdall. His hands were trembling and sweat stung his eyes, but he took three careful pictures. Then, the professional in him demanding more, he finished the roll on close-ups of the severed tail and the mangled tube of the fuselage, rounding off with a couple of shots of the general devastation. Later, when he wondered what had possessed him, he supposed it was that a sceptical fragment

14

of his mind knew it was eventually going to demand evidence. But there and then, once the camera was out, his actions were quite automatic.

It was nearly seven o'clock before he finished. A few dribbles of smoke were still rising from what was left of the mainplane and the man in the tree still looked as if he were sleeping as Brennan put his back on the scene and started for the village.

CHAPTER TWO

WELL over an hour had elapsed since the plane struck, which seemed to Brennan an impossibly long time for him to have retained exclusive knowledge of its whereabouts. In a direct line Pozoblanco was perhaps eight miles away, near enough for the crash to have been heard; possibly even witnessed. If that were so La Paz would surely have been informed. But in any case he had expected indications of a search well before this. Aircraft weren't released like homing-pigeons and left to fend for themselves. They were routed, guided, constantly in touch. And this one was bound to have been in touch with La Paz.

Soon, as if in obedience to a complaint, he heard a muffled droning in the south-east. He heard it on and off for several minutes, but though it sometimes sounded fairly close it proved deceptively so. Then it faded altogether. Through breaks in its crust he could see the forest stretching into the distance, ridged and furrowed in a motionless succession of blue-green waves, and he appreciated that even from the air, even allowing for a report from Pozoblanco, the wreck was going to take some finding. He wished now that he had started a smoke-signal, yet while the havoc was all about him it had seemed that no one could possibly miss it.

More than any one thing, the image of the body wedged in the branches of the silk-cotton tree overlaid his vision as he jarred and slithered down towards the road. Festooned creepers hung like rigging in the lofty dioramas of the forest and the lush undergrowth was exotically flowered. Parakeets fluttered in

15

the lime-coloured light and once he saw a Silver-beaked Tanager, perfectly positioned for a photograph. But his thoughts were congealed elsewhere and he hurried, less than cautious, as if lives depended on him.

He had descended seven or eight hundred feet before the intermittent droning was renewed. It ebbed and flowed as unevenly as before, but nearer, and after a while he managed to catch sight of a small spotter-plane—single-engined, high-winged. Not long afterwards it came from behind the ridge with a sudden burst of sound that brought him to a standstill. It banked sharply almost at once and started on a tight turn which took it from view, but he could tell that it was continuing to circle. Presently he glimpsed it again, levelled out and moving dangerously close to the crest. Twice more it made the self-same run, throttled right back, and when it eventually reared away and swung eastwards Brennan had no doubt whatever that its search had ended.

The road wandered somewhere in the deep valleys, as brown and cracked as an empty stream-bed. Now it was this that he looked for, willing it to appear as he wearied of the descent. The heat intensified the lower he went and his sweat stung in a score of minor cuts that shock had made him unaware of previously. The extreme tension on his nerves was slackening, yet every so often he experienced an appalled after-tremor that came near to turning his stomach over and prompted a primitive need for company.

He had begun to think that in Pozoblanco they were oblivious of what had happened after all. But some twenty minutes later, hardly had he at last debouched on to the road, than—rounding a bend—he was confronted by a party coming from the direction of the village. It consisted of six provincial policemen and a priest. To his surprise they were on foot. The priest lagged in the rear, but the person at the head of the file, a sergeant, broke into a shambling trot when he saw Brennan.

There had been a disaster. A plane had crashed on one of these hills. At dawn. Had the señor by any chance heard anything? Seen anything? . . . He was a fat, dark-skinned, middle-aged individual gone soft from too long at a desk. He looked dumbfounded when Brennan answered; more, Brennan thought, at having got his information so fortuitously than by the nature of it.

"Dead?" he echoed thickly.

"All dead."

"Are you sure?"

"Quite sure. I've just come down."

The sergeant gazed at him with unrelaxed astonishment, then raised his eyes towards the ridge. They all did, the others too, but there was nothing to be seen except the rising sweep of the forest. The crest itself was hidden from the road.

"Where were you when it happened?"

"Up there."

"At such an hour?"

"I was there all night."

Brennan didn't bother to elaborate. The priest joined them, a limping old man with deep-set eyes. He carried a canvas satchel and his faded soutane was brown with dust up to the knees.

"Everyone is dead, father," the sergeant told him. "This gentleman here has seen for himself."

The priest frowned, then crossed himself resignedly. "We started off in a truck, but it broke down. Otherwise we would not have been so late." He began using his shallow-crowned hat as a fan. "We have had to walk six or seven kilometres."

"You would have been too late, anyhow," Brennan said.

"God rest them . . . Are there many?"

"I couldn't say. I know of three, but there are certainly others. There was a fire." He let a shrug finish for him.

One of the policemen put in: "The fire was visible in Pozo-blanco."

"That is so," the sergeant agreed. "The explosion was also heard. Not by any of us personally, but it was I who telephoned La Paz. We were on the road within half an hour." He spoke as if he expected praise.

"You saw the air-search, then?"

"East of here, yes—a while ago. Too far to the east, we thought."

"Something's been over since. Right over. La Paz will have a fix by now."

17

"The road is like a snake back there, señor. For much of the way the horizon is the nearest tree, so we couldn't see much." Without relish the sergeant squinted at the ridge again. "Near the top, you said?"

Brennan nodded. "With another fifty metres more height it would have about scraped clear."

"Are you prepared to show us the place?"

"I was going to suggest it."

"*Gracias*. . . . Father?"

"I will come." The priest mopped his shabby grey head. "I must." He seemed to think Brennan was entitled to another explanation. "The doctor was not available. We left word that he should follow as soon as he could be contacted."

They started off, Brennan leading. And soon it began to seem to him that there had hardly been a time when he hadn't clambered up or down this particular hillside. The sergeant followed close behind, wheezing from the unaccustomed exertion and the burden of a slung rifle. The others trailed in their wake, but it wasn't long before the priest was lagging again. Every now and then they waited for him to catch up, and the sergeant, while he had the breath for it, used these opportunities to tax Brennan further.

Once, plucking at his sodden cotton shirt, he asked: "What sort of plane was it, señor?"

"A jet. Pretty big."

"Civil or military?"

"God knows."

Later, the question was: "You were in the forest throughout the night?" It obviously continued to worry him. "Up here alone?"

"Yes. It was too risky to start down when I'd finished."

"Finished, señor?"

"I was photographing birds. *Los colibris*."

"Ah." The holdall was studied. "Ah . . . It was just luck, then? Chance?"

"You could call it that," Brennan said.

Sometimes, while they rested, he gazed at the impassive peasant faces of the village policemen and wondered how they would react when they reached the scene; what, for instance, they would make of an apparently unscathed man perched twenty feet off the ground. It was years since he had been at close quarters with sudden death and the horror did not easily go out of him. The stench seemed still to linger in his nostrils and the boneless feel of the body he'd turned over was sickening to remember.

Their progress was slow and he was glad of it, not only because he ached in every muscle. At the third or fourth halt he sat alone and changed the film in his camera, more to occupy his mind than for any other reason. The old priest eventually dragged himself level with where they were and they gave him a few minutes' respite before going on. Glittering shafts of sunlight pierced the high green lacework of the trees. The air was as moist and motionless as in a hothouse. Butterflies sometimes broke out of the undergrowth in their hundreds and scattered like shoals of tropical fish, while there was never an end to warning bird-calls or the startled whirr of wings. But Brennan had grown indifferent to the beauty and surprises of their surroundings. By ten to nine he estimated that they were about five hundred feet from where they had to go. He called another halt and passed cigarettes round. Chance would have no more claim on him once the climb was over. Just as soon as he could he would turn about and go down again. There had been nightmare enough for one day.

"Listen," the sergeant said suddenly.

This time the engine-beat was coarser, more guttural, bearing their way with urgent certainty. They searched the ragged streamers of sky above their heads and presently a helicopter flailed over, blinking the sun. Its flight was impossible to follow without interruption, but Brennan was at least able to glimpse it swivelling into position below the crest. Hardly had it lowered itself from view than a second snarled angrily across the face of the hill and started fussing for a vertical opening. He couldn't believe that either would attempt to land. Sure enough, they presently rose again in rapid succession and made off, the great blades blurred, the thin tails canted up.

"Going?" the sergeant queried as the din diminished. "Why are they going?" He was baffled. "Is it the wrong place?"

"No," Brennan said. "I think you'll find they've put someone on the ground."

He was right. When they eventually reached the area there were at least a dozen uniformed men in possession. Some wore Red Cross armlets on their mottled battle-tunics and there was a field-radio already set up in a central position. Clearly, this was no haphazard rescue group. The person nearest them checked in mid-stride when he saw Brennan emerge into the open, eyed him warily, then called to one of his companions. The police-sergeant went forward a little way and with self-importance announced his arrival.

"Enrique Gallego from Pozoblanco. There is a priest with us."

The ascent had been hard on him and he neither looked nor sounded impressive. The man to whom he spoke had single stars on his epaulettes, but the other, now approaching, had three.

"They're from Pozoblanca, *capitán*," the first one reported.

"Is that so?" The newcomer spared the sergeant a glance of hardly-disguised contempt. He was on the tall side, swarthy, moustached, lean and hard-looking. Under the dome of his American-style helmet his eyes were rarely still, but for a long moment they lingered. "Not you, señor, surely?"

Brennan shook his head.

"It was I," the sergeant said, "who telephoned La Paz this morning." Again he cut no ice. But he continued, explaining that he had gathered his party together on his own initiative; that, but for carburetter trouble, they would have arrived a good hour ago. "Even though we knew no one had survived we obviously had a duty to make the climb. We did not anticipate your helicopters, you understand, and—"

The captain's eyes had narrowed more than the sun required. He silenced the sergeant with a gesture. "You say you knew no one had survived?"

"Why, yes."

"How did you know that?"

"The gentleman here told us so."

20

Brennan had moved a few paces away, hoping to avoid a futile inquisition. Fatigue and renewed contact with the scene made him more curt than he intended. "I was getting pictures," he said. "Bird pictures. I was in the vicinity when the crash took place. I met the sergeant's party when I was on my way to Pozoblanco and offered to guide them back. It's as simple as that."

"A photographer? — is that what you are?"

"Yes. And now, if you don't mind, I'm pulling out. I've had my fill of this place."

"There will be a few questions first, señor . . . If you please." The politeness was an afterthought.

"You'll be wasting your time. All I know is what you can see."

"But you were here, yes?"

"Down there." Brennan pointed vaguely through the slope of the forest. "Asleep. It was all over before I really knew what was happening." He launched into a brief account of what he remembered — the frenzied storm of noise, the trees going, the flash, the fire.

"But you came up to where we are now?" They were out of earshot of the others.

"Naturally."

"It was you, perhaps, who covered the two bodies?"

"Yes, I did that."

The captain thoughtfully fingered his upper lip. He then turned and spoke to the lieutenant, who nodded and started in the direction of the radio-operator. "You'd better take the priest along while you're about it," the captain called after him. He indicated to the priest that he was free to follow, and the old man plodded past him, clutching his precious satchel. The waiting policemen the captain ignored, but to Brennan he said, "You have dashed our hopes, señor. Inevitably, we believed somebody had got out alive. True, it seemed a miracle; but we could hardly have supposed that you, or anyone else, had been here before us."

Brennan shrugged. An officer with MEDICO painted on the front of his helmet was crossing the tangled swath. There were several figures bent like reapers close to the mainplane's tilted hulk; others searched among the fringes of the forest. The bodies near the tail-unit had been moved, he noticed, and there was no sign of the man in the tree.

"I see you found the other one as well," he remarked.

"Which one is that?"

"He was over there, in the big ceiba."

"Ah, yes." The captain studied his gaitered ankles. "Fantastic." There was a slight pause. "How long were you here, señor?"

"I couldn't say for sure."

"You certainly didn't miss very much. Perhaps a photographer is more observant than most?"

"I almost missed *him*." Brennan rasped his beard-stubble. "In fact, if you were to tell me I must have imagined it I think I'd believe you. I suppose that's why I took some shots of him—just to prove to myself that I wasn't sleep-walking."

The police-sergeant had come to the officer's side. "We are here to help," he ventured. "If you would direct us, *capitán*, I and my men will—"

"Later," the captain snapped dismissively. Arms akimbo, he turned to face Brennan. "You said you took pictures." His scrutiny was intense.

"A few, yes."

"This may not be to your liking, señor, but I am afraid I must ask you for the film."

The bluntness of his manner surprised Brennan almost as much as the unexpectedness of the request. "I don't quite understand you," he countered.

"The film in your camera." The captain waited. "I am asking you for it." Then, as if to soften the slight hint of menace: "It could well turn out to be invaluable to the authorities. Anything and everything to do with the disaster will be relevant to their inquiries."

"Not the kind of stuff I took."

"That will be for others to judge. But I am empowered to insist on your giving me the film."

"You're joking, of course."

"Joking? No."

For a moment or two Brennan imagined that this was his way

22

of extracting a bribe. "Are you seriously suggesting that a handful of pictures taken *after* the plane struck are going to help establish what brought it down?" He glared back. "Nonsense. . . . In any case, there are exposures on the film other than of what happened here."

"You will be given a receipt. Everything will be returned to you in due time."

"Thanks very much."

His tone was scornful. He started to walk, but the captain gripped his arm. "You underestimate me, señor. Why not be reasonable?"

Self-control wasn't normally one of Brennan's assets, but he had reached a stage where his anger was dulled by the sheer weight of tiredness. "Reasonableness is a two-way business, captain." He knocked the other's hand away. "Look," he said, "I've had a bellyful this morning without your adding to it."

"My apologies. But I assure you I mean to have what I asked for."

The policemen were staring like cattle. Brennan had a sudden sympathy for them; for the sergeant in particular. It was one thing to watch authority crudely in action; another to experience it direct. He wanted no trouble, but there were at least half a dozen experimental pictures on the film, valuable only to him, taken at varying shutter-speeds in the sepia light of the previous evening. And then, as he continued to argue, it dawned on him that he had reloaded his camera during the later stages of the climb. He was barely able to conceal his relief. As an insurance against arousing the captain's suspicions he protested two or three times more before yielding. Eventually, with simulated reluctance, he opened the holdall, quickly wound the unexposed film to an end and emptied the camera.

"Thank you, señor." The captain unzipped a breast-pocket and extracted a notebook. "Your name, please?"

On an impulse Brennan said: "Robert Brown."

He glanced at the ox-eyed policemen, wondering if he had been seen to reload: he had done it quite openly. At the moment they were inclined to be his allies, but for all he knew one of them might be in a position to try and earn himself some merit.

"Address?"

Brennan lied again: "Hotel Clara."

"La Paz?"

"La Paz."

"I am grateful to you," the captain said. He permitted himself a tight smile. "No hard feelings, señor?"

Brennan raised and let drop his shoulders. The strip of devastation in which they stood was beginning to tremble in the mounting heat. A foul waft reached them from the far end of the cul-de-sac, shaming the pettiness of the dispute.

"*Adios*," he said grimly.

His deception would come to light in time, but idiotic demands deserved farcical results. Now, however, he thought it best to go while the going was good; before the captain took it into his officious head to impound the camera and holdall as well.

"You will walk, Señor Brown? All the way to La Paz?"

"I've a vehicle at the foot of the hill."

Brennan turned heavily and went down the slope into the trees, a draining thirst consuming him. The living were as anonymous as the dead, strangers, each and every one, and there was no cause for him to look back.

CHAPTER THREE

THE Land-Rover was safely in its hide. When Brennan had dragged away the covering of palm-fronds and clambered in he sat at the wheel and smoked a steadying cigarette. It was almost eleven o'clock, but the day had somehow lost its shape: already it seemed to have stretched so far from its frenetic beginnings that the morning's assault on his nerves now reached out to include time itself.

Eleven . . . It didn't make sense. He mopped his face and neck; found his sun-glasses on the shelf and put them on. In a direct line La Paz was about forty miles away, but the anaconda of a road which linked them involved at least a sixty-mile drive

—*and* a descent to sea-level of three thousand feet or more. It would be after one before he reached the Oasis, and the prospect of a couple of hours' hard steering over rough laterite was daunting. He seemed to have shed his strength on the hill and there was a curious weakness in him, as if he had passed through a fever.

He delayed for a while before switching on, trying to unravel his thoughts. The questions that had beaten a spasmodic tattoo against his brain were still unanswered. He would have asked the captain for information if the man hadn't been so damned hostile. It struck him as slightly ridiculous that La Paz would be buzzing with news when he got there; that he would learn from the Press and radio—even, perhaps, from someone like the elevator-boy at the Oasis—which airline the plane belonged to, where it was bound, the identity of the bodies he had seen and touched at a time when he alone knew of their fate.

The faint bloom of damp which had formed overnight on the dark metal surfaces of the Land-Rover soon evaporated now that it was uncovered. A drying mist wavered above the canvas hood. Brennan smoked the cigarette through to its end before wearily reaching for the ignition-key. The engine fired first time and the sound exploded some pigeons out of a liana-draped rosewood. He reversed on to the road, then craned for a final look at the hillside, a lingering trace of incredulity helping to mould his expression. He had no qualms about having deceived the captain. As like as not nothing would come of it. And even if some zealous official took it upon himself to have him traced, a set of prints together with a flowery apology would probably suffice to compensate for the officer's loss of face. Once the film was developed all but the first few exposures could vanish for ever into the governmental maw if someone so insisted. Unlike the bright flash and blurred quiver of the humming-birds the events of the last few hours had a static, indelible quality of their own that was going to prevent them from ever quite belonging to the past. Already he sensed this, and as he swung the Land-Rover's square nose towards La Paz his mind was a kaleidoscope of which the road was only a twisting part.

Soon after passing the abandoned police truck he was cruising into Pozoblanco, a ramshackle place of pock-marked walls and thatched and corrugated roofs. The small rectangular plaza, unpaved and down-at-heel, offered a fierce dazzle of tinted façades—church, court-house, police-station—that defied the traveller to stop and stare. In any case visitors could go hang as far as Pozoblanco was concerned: it made no concessions. The Coca-Cola plaque was as incongruous as the daubed PAN-AMERICANO slogans. A skinny dog uncoiled itself from an angle of shade and ran barking into the Land-Rover's dust, but otherwise the village was in the grip of an enormous inertia. A few heads turned to follow Brennan's progress and the watchers' sullen indifference made him marvel that the sergeant should have been roused to action by anything as remote as the reported sight and sound of a distant explosion.

There was a saloon on the corner where the plaza narrowed again in to a street, its dark entrance framed by a red and white surround. Brennan braked and got out, impelled to slake his thirst. Standing on a chair inside the doorway a very thin man was languidly substituting fresh fly-papers for old.

"*Buenos*," Brennan greeted him, and ordered a beer. The response was unenthusiastic but the beer was marvellously cold. A memory prompted him as he wiped the froth from his lips. "Where can I find the doctor?"

"He is not here. And when he comes back he is wanted up in the hills—urgently. There has been an aeroplane accident. *Un desastré*." The man might have been talking about the weather. A tacky coil of paper, crusted with flies, dangled from one hand.

"You know where he lives, though?"

"Of course, but I tell you he isn't at home. He was called away to one of the *fincas* during the night."

Brennan slid a peso across the counter. "You'll be doing him a favour if you get word to him not to bother with setting out again. There aren't any survivors."

"No?"

"It'll be a journey for nothing."

The bartender leaned on a sharp elbow. "I doubt if he'll accept that from me. Why should he?" He seemed to notice nothing

26

significant in Brennan's sweaty dishevelment. "Why should he, señor?" he repeated as Brennan waved the change away.

"Because I'm just down from guiding the police-party to the wreck. There's a rescue team already up there from La Paz and it includes at least one doctor. Yours might as well save his legs."

The man looked at him with growing interest. "Everyone dead, eh? That is bad. . . . Bad. And you were there, señor? You saw them?" Now he wanted to talk, to learn more. Death was a commonplace, but in this fashion—even though it remained beyond pity—it had a certain distinction. "As sure as God made Jesus Christ, you were there? You know what happened?"

Brennan turned to leave, anxious to spare himself another chain of answers. "Tell the doctor, will you?" He was brusque again, his emotions still ragged and easily provoked.

"Naturally, señor. As soon as possible."

The bartender followed Brennan to the doorway and out under the brassy fist of the sun, belatedly proud of this chance association. The Land-Rover's door-handle was almost too hot to touch. A naked child stared from the gutter as the starter retched; some chickens scattered.

"I will see to it personally, señor."

What remained of Pozoblanco was soon gone, petering out as it had begun with squalid clay shacks set along the frayed edges of the road. The forest took over, pressing in from either side, untamed and beautiful, disgracing the injustices and apathy of men. The road began to writhe again, dipping and tossing, seeking a way through, demanding all Brennan's concentration. Sometimes it swerved between the breasts of slopes; at others it became a ledge with a sheer drop on the open side into precipitous green chasms. He sounded the horn constantly. Every blind corner demanded an act of faith, but in the first few miles his only near encounter was with a wild pig which went blundering out of sight into the underbrush.

It was almost eleven forty-five before he met the ambulances. There were three of them and he pulled out dangerously close to the brink to let them grind past. They were military ambulances, he noticed, and there was an officer beside the driver of the lead vehicle. The ubiquitous PAN-AMERICANO slogan was finger-scrawled in the dust caked along the side of the second one. This, in view of the fact that, like the others, it was American-built—a Chevrolet—seemed to Brennan akin to preaching to the converted. The island of Santa Marta was an American preserve, its government hopefully aided and abetted by the U.S. dollar. The helicopters had also been American, and practically everything else about the rescue group bore the stamp of American aid—uniforms, small-arms, accoutrements, even the ball-point of the captain in charge. Frank Merchant was always babbling about the need to stop the Caribbean rot, the necessity of 'political and economic continuity' in the area—and the bastard was probably right. He ought to know; as an Embassy man he was professionally involved. But for the love of God, Brennan thought irritably, let the dead—whoever they were—be spared someone else's aspirations.

He waited for the air to clear before driving on. Across the valley the mouldering citadel built by El Conquistador more than four centuries earlier loomed up on its overgrown volcanic heap. Nothing lasted, that was certain. The slogans had changed a hundred times since the citadel fell into decay. But one of El Conquistador's contemporaries had recorded his impressions of the island's flora and fauna, and of the humming-birds it was clear that he had seen the Princess Helena's Coquette, the Copper-rump and, very probably, the Rufous ('*a body of emerald green, brown head, cunningly mottled, wings the colour of a dove's and tail feathers that are white, scarlet and blue— the entire bird fashioned so as to be no more in length than a man's middle finger*') . . . Here was the only sort of continuity Brennan reckoned he understood. Nature had eternity to play with and could afford to be patient with its own experiments.

By twelve he was descending the escarpment, looping down in low gear by way of a dozen or so hairpins. There was a heat mist over the plain and a welding seam of cloud along the lavender horizon. He had been three weeks in Santa Marta and never a day passed without some aspect of its beauty impinging on his senses. But in his present mood they were unreceptive. The morning's trauma had not greatly diminished and the question-marks continued to drift in and out of his mind. It was unnatural to know what he knew and yet to know practically nothing. As he wrestled the wheel the knuckles of the central range panned back and forth across his rear-view mirror and he tried, almost with desperation, to push his thoughts forward, away from the plane's screaming descent and the celery snap of trees and all that had followed. More than anything he needed a bath, a few hours' sleep and a change of clothes. Then, maybe, he'd achieve some kind of perspective and pick up the threads with Alison again—beginning with the apology he owed her for not getting back to La Paz last night.

There was a small village near the base of the escarpment, its dwellings huddled abjectly together, and his passage trailed dust over them. From there on the road came down more gently out of the forest into coconut groves and rows of limes and trim cotton fields. And there was activity to be seen—men hacking arrowroot out of the ground; women winnowing chaff. It gave Brennan an increasing feeling of normality, as if a dream were at last ending, and he drove a little faster, anxious to have the journey done. A sign told him that La Paz was fourteen kilometres. Slatted hoardings began to appear along the wayside lauding restaurants, hotels, cordials, rum—writ large so that he who ran could read. The Oasis Club's was bigger than most—international cuisine, air-conditioning, swimming, tennis, seafishing . . . But at least it made a welcome change from the political stuff.

Away to his left he began getting his first glimpses of the sea, its calm so dead that the clouds were mirrored to perfection. Monterrey came and went, hugging the beaches, a weekend retreat for the very rich—thick, cool stucco walls and old-style private patios blended with glass façades and cantilevered decks. Then more open road with mango trees and royal palms along the plantation avenues, lava-black earth to either side and the cluttered mass of La Paz beginning to fill Brennan's frontal view—its traditional skyline fighting a losing rearguard with the contemporary geometry of office blocks and shopping centres. The inevitable slums came first, crouched low, foul and odorous, ignored by the guide-books and unredeemed by the occasional splash of bougainvillea or a vivid show of cannas—a wilderness of alleys and saloons and leprous stone that gradually merged with an area where tramcars clanked between rows of cheap rooming-houses and ploughed through grassless, graceless squares. The smells changed, too. The traffic increased, taxi and horse-drawn barouche, bicycle and truck; and all manner of people thronged the burning pavements, all shades of skins and degrees of purpose.

Brennan turned towards the harbour. Out there a couple of liners rode at anchor, immaculate and aloof, clear of the forests of masts and wheel-houses of hundreds of small craft along the mole and sea-wall. Beyond the harbour's curve were the glaring alabaster plazas and ornate houses of crushed shell and coral which formed the heart of old La Paz—the arcaded sidewalks, the filigreed balconies and brown-ribbed roofs, the Romanesque cathedral gone golden-grey with age.

A white-helmeted policeman delayed him at the next intersection; a red light at the one following. Only when the Land-Rover was at a standstill did Brennan feel the full throbbing pulse of the sun's heat. Past the enormous bronze statue of El Conquistador, down the wide, palm-lined avenue that led to the Presidential Palace, past the Casino and its glittering fountains and on through the strident traffic to the Oasis Club's driveway. It was well after one o'clock, nearer half past, and Brennan felt as though he had sweated himself into his seat for good and all. He slung his gear and walked across the car park, layer upon layer of weariness aching through him, dirty and unkempt, oblivious of being stared at from under the quartered umbrellas on the terrace. He went up the shallow steps into the comparative dark of the entrance lobby. The conditioned air which enveloped him seemed impossibly clean and cool. He crossed to the desk to collect his mail and then, with only a bleary and incurious glance at the letters handed him, walked through to the bar, sat heavily on the first high stool he came to and lit a cigarette.

"Señor?"

"Cognac," Brennan said.

"With siphon?"

"Straight."

He saw himself in the mirror opposite and thought: What the

hell? When the cognac came he tossed it back in one gulp and ordered another. He needed bracing. A dull fire spread slowly through him and he massaged his eyes with his knuckles; ran his hands over his beard-stubble. A florid-faced individual on the perch beside him picked up his frothing *daiquiri* and moved elsewhere, as if proximity were contagious. The cognac sparked Brennan's anger and a swift and unreasonable irritation possessed him, compounded out of stale shock and every ragged mood this endless day had forced upon him. Sod you, too. . . .

Somewhere, he supposed, there was an early-afternoon edition of *La Verdad* to be found; failing which José, the barman, would surely have heard one of the frequent radio bulletins or gleaned something from someone who had. He was in the act of finishing the second cognac preparatory to signalling for attention when a hand descended on his shoulder.

"Obviously," a dry voice said, "a photographer's lot is not a happy one."

Brennan gazed at the reflection in the mirror. "Hallo, Merchant." His expression did not change.

Frank Merchant slid on to the vacated stool and studied him with an amused smile. He was his usual dapper self—bow tie, silk shirt, fawn suit—and the overall effect was immensely disdainful.

"I was always led to believe," he mocked, "that humming-birds are extremely small creatures. Minute, even. And quite inoffensive."

"I'm not in the mood, Merchant."

"What's that you're drinking?"

"Cognac."

"Brother!"

Brennan shrugged.

Merchant settled himself a shade more comfortably; nodded towards the mirror. "They tint the glass in order to flatter the viewer, but even so you look as though you've come through several hedges backwards. I only hope it was in a worthwhile cause."

"Look, Merchant, for both our sakes . . ." Exasperated,

Brennan smashed his cigarette in an Oasis-branded tray. "Can't you take your heavy diplomatic style somewhere else?"

"I like it where I am. I like it very much."

Merchant blandly ordered a beer. José had poured it out and cut off its top with a wooden spatula before either of them spoke again. And then Brennan, with a tired gesture of appeasement, said: "That plane this morning—I was on the spot within half an hour of it crashing."

"Oh, yes?"

"I was still on the hillside three hours ago and it wasn't exactly pleasant."

"Is that so?" Merchant's smile was as meaningless as an asterisk without a footnote. "You know, I haven't a notion of what you're talking about. What plane?"

"Haven't you heard?"

"Mine's a humdrum existence. Where was this?"

"Up in the Colmillos range above Pozoblanco."

"News to me. What happened?"

Brennan told him, sparing the details, while Merchant fondled his beaded glass. He seemed less interested than Brennan would have believed possible, mostly squinting down between his splayed knees as though deliberating on the line of an imaginary putt. Eventually, when a suitable pause occurred, he drawled: "How odd that you should have been there."

"I don't see anything odd about it."

"Remarkable, then. I was never a great one at semantics."

Brennan drew a long, aggrieved breath. "I was sure you'd have heard something. After all, it happened seven or eight hours ago."

"Not a whisper." Another empty smile. "Cross my heart."

"If you'd been as close as I was you wouldn't be so bloody offhand."

"If I'd been as close as you were I reckon I'd want to forget all about it."

"Viva Pan-Americano."

"Weren't there any clues scattered about? Markings?"

"Not that I saw." Brennan's mind was suddenly filled with the scene, ugly and terrifying. Now it was the bar and the men

32

and women who lounged and gossiped and laughed in its arti-
ficial coolness that seemed unreal. He gazed sourly about him,
thinking of the macabre figure in the ceiba tree and the scarlet
pulp of what had been a living face. "It could have been one of
yours, you know. Doesn't that concern you?"

"We had nothing coming in or going out at that sort of hour
this morning."

"It might have been passing over. In any case, since when have
American nationals flown only with American air-lines?"

For the first time Merchant showed a trace of impatience. "It
so happens, Brennan, that I don't share your morbid curiosity.
Statistically, I dare say a plane crashes somewhere in the world
every day or so, and—"

"This one is down in your own backyard."

"Maybe. But it also happens that plane crashes aren't my particular pigeon."

"What is, for God's sake?"

Veins showed in Merchant's temples like a trumpeter's, but
the venom in his voice was well controlled. "Why don't you go
and get some sleep? Obviously, you could use it. I'm as sorry as
you are that some people have come to a nasty end, and I've no
doubt I'll read all about it in the papers. You've had a rough
morning—granted. You've been a Boy Scout—fine. But don't,
please, expect me to strike up appropriate music."

He buried his nose in his glass: he didn't realise it, but he
was about one sentence away from needing plastic surgery.
Raging, Brennan picked up his holdall and other paraphernalia
and stormed away. The sun hit him like a physical blow as he
stepped outside and he winced. He crossed the gravel forecourt
to the residential block and took the elevator up to the second
floor. An imagined irony almost induced him to ask the elevator-
boy what *he* knew about the disaster, but he desisted. The questions could wait: he was too done in to worry his head any more
for the time being. His antagonism to Merchant was provoked
by something deeper than curiosity about a crashed aircraft. He
knew himself well enough to realise this; recognised the
symptoms.

"Have you seen Señora Stacey recently?"

33

"Not for perhaps an hour," the boy answered.

"She went out?"

"No, señor. She came in."

His room seemed to have shrunk: enclosed spaces invariably pressed in on him when he had escaped them for any reasonable duration. It was a long while since he had eaten, but he had gone past hunger. He slumped on to the bed and got through to the desk; asked for a call at six o'clock with a copy of *La Verdad*. His mail consisted of letters from his two sponsors—*InterconTel*, acknowledging receipt of his last batch of movie film, and *Four Seasons* magazine, asking when he expected to be back in London. His equipment he packed into the bureau where he kept his money and passport, making sure to lock the drawer. Then he stripped off his shirt and sprawled full-length; again reached for the telephone. The promised bath and shave could wait, too.

"Room Eight, please."

"Señora Stacey?"

"That's right." He gazed hot-eyed at the ceiling, the zigzag of his thoughts slowing. "Alison?"

"Yes . . . Oh, it's you. When did you get in?"

"Half an hour ago . . . I'm sorry about last night. I know we didn't fix anything, but I intended to be around."

"Where are you? In the bar?" She was on the formal side, unpromisingly so.

"On my bed."

"Aren't you lunching?"

"I'm about to catch up on some lost sleep."

"You sound as if you need it. Did you get what you wanted?"

"More than that."

"Then everybody's happy."

He made a pained face. "I've said I'm sorry. I'd like to make amends this evening."

No reply.

"How about dinner? There's a lot I want to tell you." She made him wait again. As lightly as he could manage he said: "These long silences make me feel we're slowly drifting apart. Are you still there?"

"Yes."

"What d'you say?"

"To dinner?"

"That was the suggestion. Working dungarees, mind."

She chuckled then. "You win, Harry. What time?"

"Seven thirty?"

"Fine. I'll see you down below."

He rang off, making a long arm and simultaneously turning on to one side. Something hard pressed against his hip and with a grunt he flounced on to to his back again; fished from his pocked the roll of film he had avoided giving the captain. For a second or two he stared at it, yawning. To get up and cross to the bureau required too much of an effort. He felt under the side of the bed until he made contact with his shoes, then stuffed the film into the first his fingers found. Moments later his lids closed and he slid effortlessly into a sleep that was to be deep and dreamless.

The telephone buzzed promptly at six. Brennan seemed to come up from fathoms deep and the evening light broke hard against his eyes as he surfaced.

". . . in five minutes," he heard a crisp voice saying.

"Again, please."

"The paper you ordered will be with you in five minutes, señor."

"Ah."

He lay on his back. Thoughts stirred and eddied. He licked his lips, slowly coming to terms with actuality. For some inexplicable reason he felt vaguely uneasy; and the strange thing was that his uneasiness seemed to stem from some point in time before he was roused. He raised himself on to an elbow and the longer he surveyed the room the more the disquiet persisted. It was probably nonsense, but he couldn't quite rid himself of the idea that someone had been in there while he slept.

CHAPTER FOUR

HE was reasonably sure the two letters on the bureau-top had been left open, whereas one of them was now loosely folded along the creases. True, it could have folded itself; partially closed over after he had tossed it down. As far as he could judge nothing else was disturbed. He swung his legs over the side and went to the bureau. It was locked, and the key was—yes, in his trousers' pocket. Imagination? He wondered. Shirt on the floor where he had dropped it, clothes hanging neatly in the closet, travelling clock on the bedside table, shoes . . . Shoes. He bent down and extracted the roll of film. Imagination? It must be. He ruffled his hair and moved into the bathroom; blinked at himself solemnly in the mirror.

"Holy Mary, what happened to you?" he asked aloud.

La Verdad was delivered while he was shaving. He heard it come through the one-way slot by the door, but he didn't bother with it until he had showered and dried himself. Then, with a towel around his waist, he padded across the bedroom's patterned tiles and quickly scanned the front page. He was expecting a headline to catch his eye—if not the boldest, at least a second or a third lead. They were extravagantly presented, as usual, but no key words—*aeroplano, avión, desastré, accidente, tragedia, Los Colmillos*—riveted his attention. EL PRESIDENTE ATTENDS INAUGURAL MASS AT NEW BASILICA . . . FIRE DAMAGES LA GRANJA FRUIT MARKET . . . RECORD MARLIN FOR AMERICAN SPORTSMAN . . . Surprised, Brennan glanced farther down. There was nothing there either, nor on the back page, nor in the late panel. With increasing astonishment he noted that it was the three o'clock edition. For a moment he almost believed that he must have got his hands on yesterday's, but the date denied it. Friday: 19th . . . Muttering, he made a more careful search with the paper spread out on the bed. But though he covered every item, column by column, he couldn't find a single mention of the crash anywhere. Mystified, he gave up and started to dress. What *La Verdad* did with the news wasn't his concern: he didn't belong here. But for it to have totally ignored anything as sensational as what had happened that morning was beyond understanding. He was too late for the six o'clock radio bulletin —he switched on, but it was already over; now it was guitars and maraccas. With a kind of desperation he rang through to the desk, and without any preamble, said: "What have you heard about that plane that came down in the hills today?"

"Señor?"

Brennan repeated himself, but it was clear that he was wasting his time. The girl had no idea what he was talking about and, with trained politeness, told him so. He didn't press her. Outside, at roof-level, a marigold sun was burning its way through raw-edged scabs of clouds. He rang off and stood at the window, watching the bats' sunset flit but mentally occupied by the holocaust of dawn. He hadn't imagined *that*. Or the helicopters. Or the ambulances on their way up. Yet it was almost as if there were a conspiracy to make him believe so. Frank Merchant, *La Verdad*, some girl or other downstairs . . .

There was nearly an hour to kill before he met Alison. He was restless, with half a mind to seek company merely to establish that others in La Paz were aware of what he knew. But the letter from *Four Seasons* was a nagging reminder of work, and experience had taught him that it was foolish to shelve it. Self-discipline never came easily, but he opened up the bureau, sorted his colour-film and studied the previous day's log. He typed this out methodically on the Olivetti, then wrote to Benedict at *Four Seasons* saying that all being well he hoped to be in London in about a week—and would Benedict please inform *InterconTel* of this? That done, he boxed the films logged on his list and taped the package. It was ten past seven when he finished. Twenty minutes. Just long enough to have his mail registered *and* to drop the roll of black and white in at Vega's for processing. There was something quite ludicrous about wanting proof of what he had seen with his own eyes, but he was baffled enough to feel he needed it. In any case, the experimental shots of the Copper-rumps were worth having as soon as possible.

Twenty minutes . . . He left the room and made his way down to the Land-Rover. Day was done, but even so the night air seemed oven-hot after the conditioned cocoon of the past few hours. The motionless crests of the royal palms along the driveway were like shrapnel bursts against the early star-scatter and the scent of blooming pimentos filled his nostrils. Gaudy pustules of light flanked the wide Conquistador avenue into which he swung after clearing the Oasis's gate. Three minutes' judicious speeding brought him to the Post Office. At this hour the clerks were inclined to be even more languid and frustrating than was customary, but as luck would have it the man who dealt with him seemed in a hurry, too.

"Brennan?" he asked, studying the signature on the registration form.

"That's right."

"Brennan, Oasis Club." A momentary hesitation with the inking stamp, perhaps; then a dismissive nod. "*Bueno Gracias.*"

The Vega shop was only a couple of blocks away, and Brennan walked. The disquiet which had greeted him when he awoke hadn't entirely dispersed. Once, quite involuntarily, he turned his head and glanced back along the thronged pavement; though what he expected to discover he couldn't think. But this was his mood now—irritable, dissatisfied, vaguely distrustful.

He had used Vega's several times. It was by far the most reliable photographic equipment shop in La Paz, specialising in a *rapido* developing and printing service for tourists which— apart from being all it claimed—maintained an exceptionally high standard. Vega himself was a small, monkey-faced Santa Martan with a withered left arm and a formidable array of bad teeth that disfigured an almost permanent grin.

Brennan greeted him in English. "Hallo, Gabriel. Still working?"

"Twenty-four hours a day."

"I'm beginning to believe you."

"If you don't you should ask my wife." For once the shop was empty but it never did seem to shut. "What can I do for you, Mr. Brennan?"

"A straight d. and p. job. Contact prints, normal gloss finish. Can you manage it by the morning?"

"Of course. More of those magnificent birds of yours?"

"Yes and no."

"I'll see to them personally. After some of the stuff that comes in here it will be a pleasure, believe me."

Brennan nodded his thanks. "Don't be surprised at what you find. Some of them aren't pretty." He paused, as watchful as if he were making a litmus test. "They're mostly of that plane crash this morning."

"Please?" Vega queried.

"Near Pozoblanco." Brennan waited, the line of his mouth stiffening. Galled, he said: "I suppose you don't know anything about it either?"

"No, Mr. Brennan, I can't say I do. A plane crash?"

"Are you sure? You didn't by any chance hear a mention on the radio? . . . Look," he prompted, hoping he might jog Vega's memory, "it was a jet, a biggish one, and it smacked into the Colmillos hills not long before dawn. Everyone was killed— passengers, crew, the lot. An army rescue team was put in by helicopter fairly soon afterwards and ambulances were sent up from La Paz . . . Doesn't any of that ring a bell with you?"

Vega made a shrugging gesture with his sound arm. "It's the first I've heard. But then I don't take the evening paper—"

"There's nothing about it in there."

"No?" Vega's face creased into its own version of a frown. "You were present, you say? On the spot?"

"Soon afterwards. Well before anyone else. All but the first half-dozen shots will show you what it was like."

"It must have been terrible," Vega said, genuinely horrified. "Terrible. How many were killed?"

"I haven't an idea." Brennan shook his head slowly. "What beats me is that nobody I've spoken to down here is even aware what's happened."

"I'm the last person to ask, Mr. Brennan. My wife always tells me I am the worst-informed man she has ever met."

"Why nothing in the Press, though?"

"Perhaps they wish to notify the next-of-kin."

It was the first logical suggestion to come Brennan's way, yet it didn't entirely satisfy. "They needn't have named names. That could have waited."

Vega shrugged again, hand on the film. He started asking questions, the inevitable questions, the unanswerable questions, but the clock on the wall was showing seven twenty-five and Brennan explained that he had to be going.

"Tomorrow morning then, eh?"

He went out. On the corner near the shop a young, blind woman was hoarsely offering the week's lottery tickets and her desolate, milk-white stare so moved Brennan that he paused to drop a few coins into her cup. There were suddenly worse things than death; more disturbing than his own unrest. She called after him to take his ticket, thanking him with a stream of blessings when he refused. He walked quickly past a freshly-daubed slogan—VIVA SANTA MARTA—to where he had left the Land-Rover and was fortunate enough to beat all the lights on the way back to the Oasis; otherwise Alison would probably have had to wait for him.

He didn't see her arrive. The first he knew of her being there was when she said "Hallo" from about a yard away. He slid off his stool at once. Her eyes were fine and dark and her short blonde hair grew beautifully away from her forehead: this more than anything he always seemed to notice first. Tonight she was wearing a close-fitting sharkskin dress of pure white which accentuated the deep tan of her throat and bare arms. No necklace, no clip, no hand jewels; just small diamanté ear-rings. The overall effect was breathtaking and Brennan told her so.

"What are you drinking?"

"I think a *daiquiri*." She wrinkled her slightly freckled nose. "Yes, *daiquiri* and ginger ale."

"Sure?"

"Quite sure."

"Here? Or do you want to escape the place right away?"

"Here will be fine."

"I thought we might go on to *The Conch Shell*."

"Wonderful."

40

He ordered through the drift of other voices. She asked for a cigarette and leaned towards the lighter's yellow stem of flame, steadying her fingers against his.

"I didn't know you smoked," Brennan said.

"I don't often. Two or three at most. If it's more I gasp and blow next day and the client imagines his placings have come on a mile."

"Sounds like a good business ploy to me."

Merchant briefly intruded his thoughts, but he dismissed him as they laughed. Jealousy was a new experience; involved an intensity of dual feeling of which he was only just becoming aware. It was about ten days since he had met Alison. They had been in the Club's elevator together when a temporary power failure suspended them between floors. He had imagined that, like himself, she was a guest: certainly it never occurred to him that she could be the resident tennis coach. If Wimbledon was anything to go by, women tennis-players were all muscle and bounce; whereas Alison Stacey was slim and immensely feminine. It was still a mystery to him how anyone as slight and softly proportioned could produce such a man-powered overhead smash or a forehand that rocketed the ball so explosively across the net. The secret could only be timing, and if that were so it had taken her a long way in the amateur game—the semi-finals at Forest Hills when she was twenty-two, the Wimbledon quarter-finals in the following year and a place in the American Wightman Cup team. She was modest about her success and he'd had to work to get her to speak of it. And it didn't matter to her that he'd failed to react to her name: tennis wasn't an all-demanding god.

When she first dined with him she made no bones about why she had turned professional. "I'd gone as far as I was ever likely to in the amateur ranks, I guess. Anyway, the international circus-life was beginning to pall. So when the Oasis came up with this offer—I was on vacation here after the Caribbean tournaments last year—I decided it was time I started earning a living."

"No regrets?"

"Not one . . . Incidentally, don't you ever play?"

"Too old."

"You?" She had given him the puckered sort of look a line-judge receives after a doubtful call, he remembered. "How old is too old?"

"Thirty-four."

"Old enough to be my brother. Harry Brennan, I'm ashamed of you."

"So soon?"

That was last week. They had laughed then, too; but now, as they raised their glasses, Brennan found it hard to relax. His malaise hadn't shifted. More than anything he wanted to dismiss it as baseless and unreasonable, but despite Vega's remark about the next-of-kin he remained on edge; unconvinced. It seemed downright impossible that, of all those who were beginning to crowd the Oasis bar, he alone knew of the disaster. There was nothing to suggest otherwise. And yet; and yet . . . Hideous little cameos flickered in his mind, as if to justify his disbelief. A whole day ended and not a word on anyone's lips; no rumour going the rounds. A shiver of incomprehension moved his shoulders.

Alison was saying: "What happened to you last night?"

"Sorry?" He dragged his thoughts from their obsession.

"You've got the fidgets."

"Have I?" She was oblivious of his secret; he could see that. If Vega's explanation were correct there would have been nothing on the radio either. *If* . . . He said: "You remember where I went yesterday?"

"Los Colmillos."

"I finished up not far from Pozoblanco."

"So?"

He pushed his glass away. It was odd but he could have sworn his back was feeling the weight of someone's scrutiny. He glanced round, but caught no gaze; no nod of recognition.

"That's what I meant," Alison said, "by the fidgets."

Brennan shrugged uncomfortably . . . Merchant? Had he become that sensitive about Frank Merchant?

"You were talking about Pozoblanco. At least, that's as far as you'd got." Alison drew on her cigarette. "Is this going to be a riddle-game or something?"

"It's a riddle, right enough. But no game."

He told her then, slowly, carefully, leaving out nothing, choosing his words as if she were a stenographer, recounting every single thing exactly as it had happened from his moment of waking until he left the hillside and reached the Land-Rover. It took a fair time. Now and then she interjected some shocked remark or other, prompted him, made him repeat an occasional detail. There was a lengthy silence when he finished, and then she said: "My God, Harry, how awful."

"It was all of that." He drained his glass, trapping the sliding ice against his teeth. "But there's something strange about it all. Or at least I keep thinking so."

"In what way?"

"Well, for a start, the fact that it's so obviously news to you." She frowned. "I don't follow."

"Listen." Impulsively, he summoned José. "Tell me," he began—and together they watched the barman's blank reaction. No, señor. When was this? Where? . . . No, señor. "You see" —Brennan's hand-movement as he turned to Alison was a shade overwrought—"you aren't the only one. In fact I haven't met a soul in La Paz who knows what the devil I'm talking about."

"You must have spoken to the wrong people."

"Frank Merchant was among them."

"Just recently?"

"Seven or eight hours after the thing crashed. That's plenty for someone who's always on about having his ear close to the ground." A momentary bitterness overflowed. "Or is it his finger on the pulse?"

"You overestimate Frank." She looked at him defensively. "I expect he's had to wait for *La Verdad* like everyone else."

"*La Verdad*'s come and gone without so much as a mention. And the radio's followed suit."

"Are you sure?"

"I can't vouch for the radio, but I've had the paper upstairs." Her eyes widened. "Then what's your worry?"

"Huh?"

43

"How d'you expect anybody to know anything if the information hasn't been released?"

"Hell, Alison, Pozoblanco isn't exactly the other side of the world." He shook his head.

"Come on, Harry," she reproved him. "It's a terrible thing to have on your mind. Ghastly. But don't try and make a mystery out of it."

Brennan hesitated. There was more he could have said if it hadn't almost guaranteed ridicule. Against his will he continued to be inexplicably tense, disturbed by some animal awareness that eluded pinning down. "Watched? . . . Nonsense, Harry. What next, for God's sake?"—Alison's reaction wasn't hard to imagine. Yet that was the feeling, or as near to it as he could get. He made another and more determined effort to shrug the mood away: she deserved better than a melodramatic fancy.

"I'm not." He grinned a trifle sheepishly. "But—well, it's like coming back from the battlefield to find nobody's even been told there was a war. It's a bit bewildering to say the least. . . . Another *daiquiri*?"

"Not right now." She was quiet for a moment; thoughtful. As she stubbed her cigarette, she said: "What on earth possessed you to fool that captain over your roll of film?"

"It wasn't going to be any use to him."

"Maybe. But they won't like it. And you can't honestly blame them if they don't."

"Well, they can take it out on Mr. Brown at the Hotel Clara."

"Is that who you said you were?"

Brennan nodded.

"Wasn't that unwise?"

"It certainly wasn't very original."

Alison smiled cautiously. "I'm beginning to think you're a very impulsive person."

"Is that so?"

"Stubborn, too, I shouldn't wonder."

"Heh," he protested. "How about a little on the credit side?"

He matched her smile, but the nape of his neck prickled. He scanned the wall-mirror from end to end, vainly hoping to outwit someone. Who, though? . . . He couldn't believe the business of the false name had come to a head so soon. Even supposing it had, why the furtiveness? He wasn't hiding himself away. He was approachable enough, surely?

To blazes, he thought. The bar was getting on his nerves. Too much talk, too much smoke, too many people. It was no way to begin an evening.

"How about moving on?"

Heads swivelled as he walked with Alison to the door, but the stares she attracted were refreshingly blatant. The smooth still warmth of the night wrapped around them as they descended the outer steps. Brennan started towards the Land-Rover, but Alison steered him over to her own small red convertible near the residential block. He yielded with a gesture and climbed in beside her. The ignition-key was in place and he remarked: "You're very trusting."

"There's always a man on the gate," she said. "Nobody's going to drive this thing away without him seeing."

The engine fluttered, obliterating the fibrous rasp of cicadas. Brennan looked over his shoulder as they crunched along the gravel driveway. No one had followed them out, and it struck him as preposterous that he should even have checked on the possibility. He settled back in the low seat, welcoming the drag of air past his face, already feeling the tension diminish. In the avenue lumbering tramcars spat and whined against their overhead wires. Every fountain, every statue, was floodlit. Neon pulsed and Catherine-wheeled over the pavement cafés. *The Conch Shell* was down by the harbour and Alison took a route that was new to him, short-cutting through a tortuous maze of streets so narrow that anyone on foot had to press against the walls to let them pass. The atmosphere was spiced and heavy. Blocks of light fell from the doorways of pin-ball saloons and dingy bars where juke-boxes blared. Groups of soldiers roamed, looking for what they wanted.

"Local knowledge," Alison laughed.

A final bleat of the horn and they emerged into the wide, cobblestoned expanse of the quay. *The Conch Shell* was one of half a dozen eating places facing the waterfront and it was unpretentious enough to be spared most of the booze-drenched

45

vacation parties off the cruise ships. But it was gay, the food good and the band above average. They ate overlooking the water. There was no moon, but the stars were so thick and vast that the sea was like beaten silver. A twitchy, loose-limbed girl, as brown as a coffee-bean, sang with the band, and the intricate rhythms of the music and the honeyed throatiness of her voice were as potent as a drug. At last, for the first time that day, Brennan was haunted by scarcely a rustle of disquiet about the crash. More and more his thoughts were able to begin and end with Alison without distraction. The morning receded along with the elusive, niggling suspicions it had set in train. For the best part of three months he had lived out of suit-cases. Trinidad, Venezuela, Colombia, Costa Rica, Honduras—he had shuttled between them all, and nowhere until now had he been loath to move on once he had got the film and pictures he wanted. But when he danced with Alison, when her eyes held his across the table, the prospect of leaving for London within a week troubled him in a way that was as unfamiliar as were the emotions she provoked.

She was a wonderfully alive person, observant, direct, seemingly unconcerned with her attractiveness, which was striking, yet very conscious of men. It was a magnetic combination, and more than desire moved in him. Once, when she began a phrase with "Frank says . . .", Brennan experienced a pang of envy that was almost juvenile in its intensity.

"How's the famous back-hand?" he asked sourly.

"Frank's?" She was quick to read his mind. "You don't like him, do you?"

"I'm not enraptured."

"He's a nice enough guy. He grows on you."

"Speaking personally, I haven't noticed it."

"Perhaps you've a secret anti-American complex."

"Oh, sure. It's showing itself now."

"There are a lot of them about—not always so secret, either."

"Despite all that beautiful propaganda?"

"I wasn't thinking of Santa Marta."

"Where I come from practically every tenth person is a blood

46

relative of a New York policeman. Why, they even celebrate the Fourth of July."

"I thought you lived in London."

"London, Dublin . . . I do a sort of tax migration from time to time—all very legal, of course. But Dublin's really home. Where else, with a brogue like mine?"

"I like the brogue."

"A compliment at last." He made a mock bow.

"Tell me about Ireland. I was never there. I should have gone over to Dublin after my last Wimbledon, but I'd strained a tendon and was advised to rest."

"Then you don't know what you missed," Brennan said in the thickest accent he could manage. "Old Ireland now, it's just like the song says—a little bit of Heaven straight down from the sky . . ."

"Harry," she chuckled.

"You don't want any more of that, surely? Come on, tell me about Philadelphia instead. It rained the only time I was on my way through and I can't believe it's always so depressing."

The band played on and the singer crooned her little songs of joy and separation. Knots of people drifted in and out. Small craft moved almost imperceptibly across the shimmering bay and a ripe melon moon came up. They stayed at *The Conch Shell* until midnight, then went in the car to Sunset Point. It was immensely quiet amongst the palms and twisted divi-divi trees, and the trembling lights of La Paz seemed as remote as the stars themselves. The dull, regular fall of waves on the ghostly arc of beach below marked off the passage of the night. Alison had a style of kissing, of repeatedly brushing her lips along the line of his, that was sensual in the extreme, but always she finally pushed Brennan gently away, leaving him torn between longing and uncertainty. He didn't demur. She had driven to Sunset Point without prompting, without a word being said, but neither out of habit nor because she felt it was his due. He was sure of this. Her mouth he knew, the softness of her hair, and the pressure of her lithe body. But she was strangely shy. There were limits beyond which he could not go. His vanity may have suffered, but deep down he was glad, relieved. He had never been in love before, but these were the first intimations and they were as heady as her scent and the taste of her skin. The moon floated high into the dark crests of the palms and La Paz gradually lost its opulent, midnight sparkle. They had talked so much, discovering one another, but even the silences seemed to increase his knowledge of her and by the time she said she had to go he flattered himself that there was more than cautious affection in her last kiss.

"I'm on court at ten," she said, using the pull-down mirror. "With all the sleep I'm going to get I can see him giving *me* the lesson."

"Him?"

"Frank."

"He needs his head seeing to."

"It's not too hot until about eleven or so. Anyhow, Frank's well acclimatised."

"Doesn't he ever do anything in that Embassy of his?" That she always defended Merchant made him unreasonably caustic. "Or is he mostly out at night with a paint-pot and brush?"

"I've no idea how he's organised."

Alison switched the head-beams on and a moth found them within seconds. They bumped slowly down the track which led to the coast road, then accelerated away towards the city. They had reached the tram terminus, silent and deserted now, before either of them spoke again. Then Alison said: "Are you going to be at the Presidential Reception on Sunday?"

"Not that I know of."

"Have you applied?"

He shook his head. "Will you be there?"

"Yes."

"How do I go about it?"

She swung out to pass a man who dozed astride a plodding donkey. "I believe application has to be made to one's Cultural Attaché, but I'm not really sure. Frank fixed it for me."

"Oh."

"It's a lot of fun. A monumenal waste of money, God knows, but a whole lot of fun. I've been once before." The Casino was

48

off to the right and there was life there still. "Do come, Harry," she said.

"I doubt if they'll let me in. I haven't the clobber."

"What's 'clobber'?"

"Cockney for clothes. I'm a working lad, remember. Besides, there isn't an Irish Consulate or what-have-you on the island. And though we have reciprocal arrangements with the British, they're on what they're pleased to call a courtesy basis. I can't quite see myself making the British list when they've surely been cutting their own gentlemanly throats to get on it themselves."

"Frank could maybe fix something for you as well."

"No thanks."

She sighed. "I might have guessed."

"Sorry. But he brings out the worst in me."

They were passing Vega's, closed at last. Gangs of men were hosing down the deserted streets and there were rainbows in the fine spray hanging under the lamps. Brennan said: "I'll have a shot with the British tomorrow, though I reckon it's pretty late in the day." Then, flippantly: "Perhaps I could also apply as Mr. Make-Believe Brown, false beard and all, and double my chances. What d'you say?"

He saw Alison frown. "I wish you hadn't done that . . . Truly," she added, and her seriousness surprised him. "You're a long way from home. You don't want trouble. It's not just your having given the wrong name. It's the switch you did."

"Well, it's done now."

"They can be awfully touchy."

He shrugged. "They're welcome to all the prints they want if it really worries them, though for the life of me I can't imagine what purpose they'll serve. Come to think of it, I reckon that if I were formally to present a set to the authorities I'd pretty well guarantee myself an invitation for Sunday's junket. You know? —for services rendered."

Alison steered into the Oasis's drive, the gate-warden yawning as they passed. It was well after two. They walked across to the residential block and took the elevator up to the second. "Good night, Harry," Alison said. "It's been wonderful."

"How about lunch tomorrow?"

"Aren't you off somewhere?"

"Not any more. I'm in temporary retirement until about next Wednesday."

"And then?"

"Home, I suppose."

For a fleeting duration she showed dismay; enough to hearten him. "I can't believe it."

"It's true, I'm afraid." He hesitated, and the moment passed. "Lunch, then?"

"Of course." She touched his cheek lightly with her fingers. "Good night, and thanks again."

Tired though he was, for a longish while Brennan could not sleep. And when at last he went under he dreamt that he was writing to Benedict, explaining that he must delay his return by at least a week. The dream eventually moved out of him and another entered in—though he remembered neither when he first woke. In this second dream he found himself standing by the silk-cotton tree on the edge of the swath made by the plane and staring up at the figure lodged in its thick branches. Rigid with shock he heard himself call: "Are you all right?" and to his consternation the man answered, though what he said was unintelligible. Brennan stepped nearer. "Are you all right?" he repeated hoarsely, and again the man answered, more distinctly this time but in a delirium of language that Brennan neither understood nor even recognised. Then, as the dream disintegrated, the eyes closed in the plump, grey face and the cropped head fell sideways so that there was no chance, either way, of finding out more.

CHAPTER FIVE

SANTA MARTA's principal daily, *El Nuevo Mundo*, carried a couple of paragraphs about the crash. They were reasonably prominent, middled in the third column of its front page, and

Brennan read them eagerly through as soon as he came downstairs.

AIRCRAFT DISASTER

No Survivors in Los Colmillos Catastrophe

Early yesterday morning a transport aircraft of the Santa Martan Air Force plunged into the hills above Pozoblanco. The plane was completely destroyed and the crew and nine passengers—civilian technicians attached to the Air Force—were all killed. An explosion was heard in Pozoblanco and some people there reported having seen a fire. An Army rescue team was flown in immediately from Alameda airfield and ambulances subsequently went to the scene from the capital.

The aircraft was on a routine domestic flight when the disaster occurred. An official inquiry is proceeding.

Less could hardly have been said, yet what was there was accurate enough in so far as his own knowledge went. It also disposed of all the plaguesome question-marks. Moreover, it rid him of yesterday's baffled sense of mystery. Indeed, his ability to have invested the lack of news with sinister implications looked somewhat ludicrous in retrospect. His nerves must have been even more frayed than he'd realised. It seemed that Vega's explanation had been right after all, and if a mere two paragraphs were inadequate for so terrible a drama—well, floods and heavy loss of life in Thailand had earned no more space, and a murderous riot in Algiers only a few lines. For *El Nuevo Mundo*'s readers there was presumably sufficient suffering and potential calamity in every day that passed to reduce interest in tragedies that befell others. More to their front-page liking were the activities of President López—off to his mountain retreat 'for consultation with Armed Services commanders' after attending Mass at the new Basilica, statistics showing increased sugar and rum exports to Europe, and a Russian astronaut's long-winded message to his American counterpart ('Peace is our profession').

The residential-block at the Oasis was always more fully booked at week-ends. Oil-field executives, planters and their families, provincial business folk, a sprinkling of military and air force officers from outlying bases—Brennan could only guess who they were. Normally, he supposed, they invaded La Paz to shop, bank, go fishing, play golf, tour the fleshpots: but today practically every seat in the breakfast-room was occupied. There were also more women in evidence than usual and he put it down to the lure of the Presidential Palace on Sunday. Alison wasn't among them, but since it was well after nine thirty before he put in an appearance he imagined that she had already come and gone in readiness for her ten o'clock session on court.

It was too soon in the day to begin worrying his head over Frank Merchant. If there had to be a reason for his dislike of the man it could only be that Merchant would be in La Paz and using the Oasis long after he had gone. He had met him, barely a week ago—Alison introduced them—and though Merchant's endless blah about keeping Santa Marta 'on course' and his patronising raillery had got under Brennan's skin almost from the start, it was really during the past thirty-six hours that he had begun to feel so strongly about him.

He ate at a table with an expatriate Spanish citrus-grower from the far west of the island, a voracious individual with hairy wrists and a blue-glazed jowl who clearly wasn't in the mood for talking. From previous mornings Brennan recognised a few people in the room and there was someone not far away who seemed to think he knew him; at least, Brennan a couple of times just intercepted the tail-end of a sidelong glance, or believed he did. Yesterday he would have been on edge enough to attach significance to it, but sleep and the report in *El Nuevo Mundo* had erased his disquiet. Nor could he share Alison's concern over his having duped an officious uniformed bureaucrat.

He read the two paragraphs through again. The captain, he recalled, had said: "Anything and everything to do with the disaster will be relevant to the inquiry"—something of the sort, anyway. Yet here it was stated that the official inquiry was already proceeding. He smiled a trifle cynically. So much for Santa Martan thoroughness if he, the key witness, hadn't been run to earth or appealed to to come forward. Not that he could have contributed anything useful. The moments immediately prior to the crash were a shrieking blur, vivid and indestructible; but value-less. And what his camera had recorded had been seen by a score of people besides himself. It seemed that chance had done with him, once and for all.

He nodded farewell to the citrus-grower and went outside to the Land-Rover. The whanging sound of a hard-struck tennis ball reached him from the other side of high laurel hedges and he thought: You bloody maniac . . . It was ten fifteen and the sun was already doing its best to gut the strength out of the day. He topped up the radiator and drove into the world of flags and statues and slogans and other bolsters of hope. Opposite the British Embassy two cars were locked like stags, bumper to bumper, and a crowd had gathered while the drivers swore and gesticulated at one another. He found a space and parked close by. A grey-haired man was watching the proceedings from the Embassy's first-floor balcony and he grinned as Brennan mounted the steps—a grin that was like a password. On opposite walls of the vestibule were an atrocious chocolate-box oil of the Queen and a framed map of the British Isles which showed Eire in outline only, as if everything south of the border were undis-covered country. It was enough to kill whatever optimism he might have had. A dazzling olive-skinned receptionist at a desk beneath the central chandelier interrupted her manicure to sug-gest that it was a Mr. Cooper Brennan should see. One flight up, turn right, the name was on the door. . . . He thanked her and climbed the wide, L-shaped staircase. A discreet plate read: Mr. Charles Cooper. Brennan knocked, waited, then went in, to find himself in a large all-white room with a churning fan and floor-to-ceiling windows flung wide. The clamour of fierce argument rose from the street. Outside on the balcony was the shirt-sleeved man who had grinned at Brennan minutes earlier. Now he came in, shaking his head, grinning still.

"God, what a lot they are! If it weren't that I had work to do I could spend my day out there. On the face of it it's one big music-hall turn." A King Charles spaniel unexpectedly padded through the window and came smelling at Brennan's legs. "George," the man said, "behave yourself. George! . . . It's un-canny, you know, but he always recognises someone from home.

Never fails." The spaniel moved away and subsided under the fan, tongue lolling. "He's rather good, you know. Wasted out here. They have the most terrible mongrels with heads like wolves . . . I'm sorry," he went on, extending a hand. "Mr—?"

"Brennan."

"Charles Cooper." He had a half-throttled sort of voice, a flush rather than a tan, the palest blue eyes Brennan had ever seen. "How can I help?"

Brennan explained who he was and mentioned Sunday night. Cooper spread his hands.

"Can't oblige you there, I'm afraid. Wish I could. We're pretty severely rationed as regards our own nationals—and, well, putting it not too nicely, Mr. Brennan, you don't exactly qualify."

"I quite understand."

"Damn pity, but there it is. Our final list went in days ago, anyway." He brushed the spaniel's rump with a foot. "You won't be missing much, believe me. I'd prefer a decent steak and a bottle of wine any time."

A whistle sounded in the street. Instinctively, Brennan followed Cooper on to the balcony. A trio of policemen were making frantic efforts to disperse the crowd pressing round the interlocked cars. There was a great deal of fierce pushing going on and the drivers had already come to blows.

"It frightens me, sometimes," Cooper said. "Everything culminates in chaos. They're manacled to it. And it isn't always so funny. Have you been here long?"

"Three weeks."

"Staying?"

"Only a few days more."

"I envy you." Cooper sighed. "A month's about long enough. You'll be spared the disenchantment. The fruit's quite rotten under the skin, you know. Absolutely, stinkingly rotten. God, it's sad. The tourist may be delighted, but the sociologist is appalled and the political observer despairs. . . . What d'*you* do?" He had this way of taking refuge in a question, as though he found it embarrassing to unburden himself.

"I'm a photographer."

"How very interesting." The street-scene was forgotten. "People? Places? Wild life?"

"Wild life would about cover it."

Cautiously: "*The Field? . . . Country Life?*"

Brennan smiled. "Not for some while."

More cautiously still: "*H. Brennan?*"

"Guilty, I'm afraid."

"Well, I'll be damned." Cooper wheeled enthusiastically into the room. "And surprised. I somehow thought of you as an older man."

"I'll take that as a compliment."

"My dear fellow, it's just that I seem to have seen your work —on and off—for years. What brings you to Santa Marta?"

"Humming-birds, mainly."

"Fascinating."

"It's the sort of work that makes me a perpetual tourist, though."

"None of the burning Irish political and social conscience?"

"Not so as you'd notice."

"You must be unique, Mr. Brennan."

They both laughed. Brennan shook hands. "Forgive me for taking up your time."

"Not at all. I'm only too sorry I can't help over the posh party tomorrow." At the door, Cooper said: "I'm delighted to have met you. Delighted. And if there's anything I *can* do, don't hesitate to get in touch. The snag is that until you abandon that green passport of yours there's damn-all assistance I'm empowered to offer—unless you're in some fix or other. And much as I hope we meet again I wouldn't wish trouble on you, least of all in Santa Marta." The spaniel wagged its tail sluggishly. Cooper's parting words were: "It's a terrible waste having him here, don't you think?"

A crinkled smile and the door closed. Brennan went slowly down the stairs. The receptionist glanced up from her scarlet finger-nails to flash him a far from demure look. Outside, the heat was beginning to bounce off the tarmac and the sharp-edged shadows were as black as Indian ink. The crowd had largely cleared from the two cars, but the drivers seemed to have joined forces and were now remonstrating with the police. Chaos was right. As he climbed into the Land-Rover Brennan glanced back at the Embassy's Colonial-style façade. Cooper was on his veranda again and he cut a strangely remote and ineffectual figure, somehow withdrawn from the harsh realities of the world he so deplored.

A teeming tram crashed by, threatening to shake off its hangers-on, and Brennan nosed into the traffic's stream. Disappointment can only follow expectation and he hadn't seriously hoped the Embassy would be able to do anything, particularly at so late a stage. Receptions and the like weren't much to his taste, anyhow, and but for this one meaning that Alison was going to be inaccessible for an entire evening he wouldn't have so much as tried for an invitation. He turned into the Avenida del Conquistador and headed for Vega's. Perhaps because Cooper's remarks were fresh in his mind he seemed to notice more of the city's ugliness, more scabrous alleys just off the palm- and flower-lined thoroughfares, more extremes of flashy wealth and the hard life, more signs of inhibiting force—police, mitiamen. He remembered the story from somewhere of the foreigner approached by a native who asked the classic question: "Would you like to sleep with my sister?" and the foreigner's reproachful reply: "I can't even drink your water." VIVA SANTA MARTA, the daubed slogans read, VIVA PAN-AMERICANO, and he thought of Merchant and his finger-wagging references to Cuba; then—as so often—of the lush green mountains beyond the plantation-landscapes and how they shamed man's corrupt and desperate condition. He hadn't been entirely honest with Cooper, but he was too much of a nomad for his conscience to have fed for long on any one piece of soil.

A wobbling cyclist slowed him down as he approached Vega's. He drew carefully into the kerb near the blind ticket-seller, anticipating Vega's cheerful, monkey-faced greeting, eager to see the developed prints. Normally, no matter how crowded the shop, Vega was never too busy to spare him at least a welcoming nod; but today was an exception. There were only three customers there—an outlandishly-garbed vacation couple availing themselves of the *rapido* service, and someone busy making a selection of colour-slides from a revolving display.

"Morning, Gabriel."

Vega seemed to notice him with reluctance. "A few moments, Señor Brennan."

It was a brusque reply, almost hostile, and so out of character that Brennan was more than surprised. Inexplicably, tension was conveyed. He felt it immediately, but couldn't for the life of him grasp why this should be so. He watched Vega fussing over the couple's order. Outwardly the little man was as attentive as usual, but he twice made errors—once when he dated a receipt-slip and a second time over some change. It wasn't like him. Tired out? A row with his wife? . . . None of the excuses Brennan put forward on his behalf seemed adequate. He waited, unable to escape or justify a slight quiver of foreboding. When the couple eventually came to leave, Vega's belated smile was a travesty.

"Am I next?"

"Please." He was sweating, Brennan noticed, and for some reason he used Spanish. "The other gentleman will be a little time."

Straw-hatted, panda-eyed behind dark glasses, the person referred to seemed too engrossed with the battery of colour-slides to notice that he was under discussion, but Brennan murmured *"Gracias"* as he stepped forward, drawing the briefest of glances, an abstracted shrug, by way of response. To Vega he said: "What's the matter, Gabriel?"

"Matter?"

"You aren't your normal bright self this morning. What is it?—a touch of fever?"

"Thank you, but I am well." Spanish again, and the same nervous curtness. Vega licked his lips; hesitated. "I am very afraid there has been a mistake about those prints of yours, Señor Brennan."

"Aren't they ready?"

"Something else. I don't know what to say. Such a thing can happen, but with you I should have thought it was impossible."

"Oh?"

57

"You can't have wound on, Señor Brennan." It was let drop like a stone.

"Nonsense."

Vega maintained his gaze with difficulty.

"Nonsense. Of course I wound on."

"Either you didn't or you brought in the wrong roll of film."

"What?" An intense irritation swept Brennan. "Are you telling me that I took thirty-six shots in a row and never wound on once? . . . Balls," he snapped. "Let me see them."

"There's nothing *to* see," Vega protested. "That's what I am saying."

"Show me."

Vega fumbled under the counter with his sound hand, muttering "It is most unfortunate" and similar inadequacies. He produced a folder, but his fingers were shaking so that he couldn't open it and Brennan grabbed it from him. There were six strips of negative, five of them totally blank, the other also blank except for one completely obliterated frame. In quick succession Brennan held them against the light, dumbfounded and disbelieving.

"They can't be mine," he said flatly.

"They are, Señor Brennan. I was shocked, I can tell you. Amazed."

In disgust, Brennan tossed the strips down on to the counter. "Look," he said. "I had about half a dozen of some birds—f8 at three different speeds: a thousandth, a five-hundred and a two-fiftieth. My log's back at the Oasis, but I don't need to check. I remember damn well. . . . And I finished off the roll on the crash." He paused. "Hell, Gabriel, this is ridiculous. Just bloody ridiculous."

"Whatever has gone wrong, Señor Brennan, I can assure you that no mistake was made here."

"It must have been."

"No." Vega was agitated but adamant. "No."

"I might behave like a ham-fisted amateur once in a while, but not thirty-six times in succession."

There was an uncompromising silence, during which the customer farther down the counter turned the display of colour-slides. Brennan found himself lighting a cigarette; angrily fingering the useless strips of negative. He had particularly wanted those first few prints. The look he gave Vega was indignant and accusing.

"I'm not a kid with his first box Brownie, Gabriel. Thirty-six in a row? —and on two separate occasions? Is that what you're expecting me to swallow?"

"The winding mechanism could be faulty."

Scornfully, Brennan shook his head.

"What else can I suggest?"

"Who handled the work?"

"I did. I said I would and I did. I was here until midnight, Señor Brennan, on account of your wanting it this morning."

Another silence. Beads of sweat pimpled Vega's lined forehead and he glanced uneasily along the counter as if ashamed that someone should be witness to an argument that questioned his truthfulness. The murmur of traffic reached them; the ticket-seller's hopeless cry from the corner.

"Do you think I lie to you?"

Brennan's shrug had the effect of a tree felled across a road. Impasse. They could wrangle until nightfall and establish nothing. And there was no redress. With a display of petulance he flicked the negative-strips across the counter-top.

"I'm not paying—that I do know."

He walked away without another word. The door-carillon sounded an infuriating peal. Outside, he paused and glanced back, caught in a momentary postscript of bitterness. What sort of fool was he thought to be? Vega was mopping his face and the other person was speaking to him from his place by the colour-slides—not with the sympathy or derision of an erstwhile eavesdropper, but sidelong; covertly. And all at once Brennan felt more than burning resentment. As he made for the Land-Rover a clammy tentacle of suspicion fastened ominously round his heart.

CHAPTER SIX

IMAGINATION had played him false before. Or had it? He sat behind the wheel, the sun coming red through his closed lids, and tried to take stock. One thing was certain: he had no more botched three dozen pictures than anybody had put a bomb on the moon. Until seconds ago he'd believed Vega had accidentally ruined the film and was afraid to admit it—let the light in, confused his tank-procedure; hastily sought to cover himself with lies and crude substitution. But now . . . Yesterday there had been a feeling of someone having entered his room. Yesterday he'd sensed that he was under scrutiny. His mind whirled, thronged with dawning queries. It seemed imbecilic to suppose that he was in some way involved with anything sinister, yet his uneasiness was an extension of every inexplicable qualm experienced the previous day.

Without doubt, Vega had lied. The camera had been correctly used and there was no possibility of his having been given the wrong film. But there might not have been an accident, after all. Substitution, yes; but not an accident.

Another wave of anger rose in Brennan, goading him to go back and contact Vega. But caution whispered. Irrational fancies had disturbed him, on and off, ever since his return to La Paz—and *El Nuevo Mundo* seemed to have made a nonsense of them. Even so, this one was less vague; more reasonably founded. Was it altogether inconceivable that Vega had been under duress? Who was that other person?—patient and self-effacing beneath a straw hat . . . His thoughts whirled vainly on, smarting with pique, confused and baffled by questions and answers of his own making. Irritably, he flexed his shoulders to lift the shirt away from the skin. If they were so intent on getting their hands on his shots of the crash, why in this fashion? "They': anonymous, ubitiquitous 'they'. And always 'if' . . .) Why not a direct approach? Last evening, at the bar, he had asked the self-same thing; but now he went farther, his suspicions narrowed down. What could his camera have carried away from Los Colmillos that needed retrieving by furtive, roundabout means?—needed retrieving at all, in fact? Some poor devil blasted freakishly into the branches of a tree?

Something slowed his mind for an instant, then the brake was off again and he was nowhere near knowing what it had been. He opened his eyes and frowned through the windscreen, weighing instinct and reason, powerless to believe or disbelieve, constant only in being unable to forgive an infuriating loss. Traffic passed in swift-moving gaggles, released by the lights farther along the avenue. The pavements were crowded with people intent on destinations and from the dwindling patch of shadow on the corner the blind woman offered them luck. Brennan screwed round for another look at Vega's, but he couldn't see into the shop. His glimpse of dumbshow had been of the briefest, his disquiet equally short-lived, yet out of them he had fashioned a wild surmise; one, moreover, that stubbornly refused to be shifted.

A rough voice said: "Is this your vehicle?"

Brennan had watched the policeman approaching only a moment earlier, but it had never occurred to him that he was the intended victim. Turning, he nodded, "What about it?"

"Your vehicle?" the policeman asked him again, as if none too sure of Brennan's intelligence.

"I'm not in the habit of sitting in other people's."

"Papers, please."

Brennan produced and parted with them. There were two stripes on the man's sleeve: under the white-domed helmet his sweaty jowl was like earthenware, his eyes reptilian.

"You rent it," he announced, making it sound like a crime.

"That's right."

"You didn't say that."

By an effort Brennan held his tongue. A brown hand with scarred knuckles descended confidently on the door.

"You live in La Paz?"

"No."

"A visitor?"

"Yes."

"It is forbidden to park here."

"I didn't know."

"No?"

"I didn't know," Brennan repeated. "How could I? There aren't any signs."

The man waited, sure of himself, sure of the pesos that would persuade him to forget. But when none was forthcoming he seemed disconcerted and straightened up.

"Where does it say I can't park?" Brennan asked, calling the bluff.

"It is common knowledge."

"Common knowledge needs time to acquire."

"It is an offence, all the same. Ignorance is no excuse."

"What d'you propose doing about it, then?" There was hesitation, so Brennan pressed him, loathing the complacency with which authority was abused, feeling cheated and perturbed enough without this. "I'm in a hurry, so make up your mind."

Some passers-by stared, curious to see a foreigner so attended. The policeman swallowed, chagrined by failure, unsure of his ground. Normally a bribe was automatic; as certain as death and taxes. He resorted to a face-saving formula. "I have warned you. Another time I will not be so lenient. It is not permitted to park here—remember that, señor."

Brennan stuffed the papers into his wallet and drove away, his mood inflamed. He was beginning to hate La Paz and whatever corrupt and underhand glue held it together. The tyres made a soggy hum on the hot tarmac and it was almost impossible to decipher the traffic-lights in the glare. He took the direct route back to the Oasis, brooding over what had happened at the shop. As soon as he arrived he went up to his room and checked his log and the camera's winding mechanism. They merely confirmed his certainty that Vega had tried to fob him off with a naïve piece of rubbish—and the more the insult festered in his mind the more obvious it seemed to him that the little man had been forced into putting such a preposterous explanation forward. Thirty-six in a row! He must have known Brennan wouldn't believe him; no professional could have done, and not many amateurs, either. Yet he had been loyal to the deception to the last. "Do you think I lie to you?"

What else?

Why, though? . . . There seemed only one conclusion, persistent and baffling.

Brennan sluiced his face and went downstairs. It was eleven thirty and the bar was already in demand, but he didn't enter. Four uniformed U.S. Marine sergeants from the Santa Marta training camp at Merida were standing in the lobby, trying to decide whether to go or to stay. They were obviously new to the island and their pink faces gave them an incongruous look of innocence. Brennan always flinched a little as he came out under the sun—as if he were passing through an invisible arch just a fraction too low for him. There was no sound from the tennis-courts. He made towards the swimming-pool; saw, above the privet, someone launch himself off the high board and plunge with spread arms to apparent destruction.

Yesterday, at the post-office, the clerk had behaved as if prompted by belated recognition. "Brennan? Oasis Club?" He remembered now—the quick glance, the momentary hesitation with the inking-stamp; neither quite normal. Was there a connection with what had happened at Vega's? Had Benedict's package been set aside for subsequent investigation? Re-alerted, his imagination was on the loose, ferreting indignantly in a maze of speculation.

The privet hedge gave way to beds of lilies and showy cannas; then to a paved area of green and gold mosaic and tub-planted ferns. The pool was kidney-shaped, off-centre, but an oval ring of palms provided a sense of symmetry. Pastel-coloured dressing-room blocks stood back from tables, cane chairs and white-fringed umbrellas, and as always to Brennan the intense blue of the water looked as unreal as in a brochure read on a winter's day. The air seemed a trifle cooler and he moved nearer and filled his lungs, gazing round for Alison.

"Over here!"

It was Merchant, and though he was expecting to find him with her he felt a prick of annoyance. He located them across the pool and started negotiating a score of tables and as many prostrate forms. A girl more naked than most suddenly held her nose and pitched off one of the lower boards: the water caved, spattering Brennan with heavy blobs as it closed over her. Someone laughed and he grimaced ruefully, arming his face dry.

"Watch out for flak," Merchant called.

A waiter passed with a clinking tray-load. High, very high, an aircraft was droning over, and for an instant the aggrieved and puzzled part of Brennan's mind fastened on to it.

"Hallo, Harry," Alison was saying.

He slid into a chair. "You look cool enough."

"You're overdressed." This was Merchant. "It's bad for the blood."

Brennan glanced down at himself. Sweatshirt and denim trousers. "Maybe you're right," he conceded grudgingly, "I've been into town."

"How about a beer?"

"You're a mind-reader. Thanks."

Merchant was already smoking; Alison shook her head. Brennan lit a cigarette and drew on it deeply. "How'd the session go?"

"Fine," Alison said. "Frank's coming on like a house on fire."

She was a delight to look at—long, agile legs, firm without being muscular; lithe, small-breasted body; tanned skin gartered with white at the thighs where her shorts had ridden up.

"Did you stop by at the Embassy?" she asked.

He nodded.

"Well?"

"It's not on."

"Oh damn," she said. "Frank, can't you do something about Harry?"

" 'Do something'?"

"For tomorrow night."

"Ah." Merchant stared across at Brennan with mocking amiability. "The great tomorrow night." He lolled in the cushioned cane chair, tough, veined arms, meaty shoulders, hairy legs, bald knees. Sweat was showing along the thick hairline and in the creases under his chin, but he was as immaculate as ever— monogrammed shirt and all. "D'you particularly want to go?"

"No," Brennan said.

"Harry!" Alison protested.

Brennan shrugged. Merging vapour-trails caught his eye, dragging his thoughts back to the source of his discontent.

"You really ought to get yourself an Embassy of your own," Merchant yawned.

Brennan rode it as best he could. "Embassy or no Embassy, it's too late."

"Is it, Frank?"

"Didn't you hear?—the man doesn't want to go." Merchant tossed a palmful of nuts into his mouth; chewed reflectively. "But if he does—if he *really* does—I dare say something could still be arranged."

"No, thanks."

A bored gesture. "It's up to you."

"More aid for the underprivileged?" Brennan snapped. "When are you—"

He broke off, more angry with himself than with Merchant. A scarlet-sashed waiter brought his beer and withdrew. Hilarious shouting came from the other end of the pool. An enormously-paunched man with a cavernous navel plodded heavily past as if in pursuit of his stunted shadow.

"Sorry," Brennan growled. Merchant was an irritant in his own right, but twice now he had exacerbated another. "I've just had a row over at Vega's and I haven't come off the boil yet." He turned to Alison. "You know those pictures I told you about last evening?"

"Yes."

"Vega's bitched them up. That's not what he says, of course, but the result's the same."

"All of them?"

"Apparently I didn't wind on. How d'you like that?" He flicked ash. "Thirty-six on the film and I'm supposed not to have wound on once."

Merchant said: "This is Santa Marta, Brennan."

"So?"

"So you learn to get used to that kind of thing. They're like kids with new toys."

"Vega's a cut above the average in that respect."

"Mistakes happen."

"Not this time."

Alison's forehead puckered. "What do you mean?"

"I think I was deliberately palmed off with a set of failures."

"Deliberately?"

"I'm damned sure, in fact."

"Fighting words," Merchant drawled.

Brennan stifled resentment by grinding his cigarette in the tray. Merchant would belittle everything he said: he knew that in advance. Yet he couldn't keep his suspicions battened down any longer.

"Go on, Harry," Alison prompted.

She, at least, would listen. "Look," he said. "This may sound a lot of cock and bull, but—well, ever since I got in from Pozoblanco yesterday I reckon I've been watched. On and off, anyhow."

Merchant rolled his eyes. "Brennan, Brennan."

"You didn't exactly help. But if there's one thing I hate it's being made a monkey of without knowing why."

"Are you suggesting that Vega's a frustrated ornithologist or something?"

"You know damn well I'm not."

"I don't, you know. A clue would help—just to point me in the right direction."

"I'm suggesting that I was deliberately denied my own pictures." Brennan paused. "And, if I'm right, it can only be because they were of that plane."

"You've been reading the wrong kind of books. Be sensible, man. Why should anyone want pictures—your pictures, I mean, splendid though they undoubtedly were—when there was every opportunity of taking others?"

"That's precisely what I want to know." Brennan's eyes narrowed. "As a matter of interest, since when have you been aware that I photographed the crash?"

With a disarming gesture, Merchant said: "Alison mentioned it." He seemed a trifle put out; glanced at Alison as if for confirmation.

She nodded. "I don't know how it came up, Harry. I guess it was because I still had that 'Mr. Brown' business of yours hanging about in my head."

"You've heard about that as well, then?"

"Yes," Merchant admitted.

"You've advanced since yesterday."

"Only as far as what was in the morning paper."

"Plus what Alison told you."

"You took the words right out of my mouth."

"And you still don't see any link between that and what happened at Vega's?"

"Not as you infer it."

"Or the fact that I've been followed?"

" 'Fact'? . . . Come, now."

"Suspicion."

"I don't happen to be blessed with your creative imagination, Brennan, so how can I say?"

They were growing angry again; restraint ebbing. Alison leaned forward. "What's this about being followed, Harry?"

"Last night. It wasn't being followed so much as watched."

"When I was with you?"

"Early on. It didn't last. I'll admit I wasn't too sure."

Merchant said acidly: "And now you are?"

"I also have an idea that my room was searched, and I wouldn't mind betting my outgoing mail's been tampered with."

"Anything else?"

"Only that there's someone sitting about five tables away at this very moment whose eye I caught a couple of times at breakfast this morning without his wanting me to."

Merchant exploded forcibly: "God, it's marvellous, isn't it? . . . You're a case, Brennan."

But Alison was more reasonable. "The one with a magazine?"

"Yes."

"Marvellous," Merchant repeated, tossing his head. "Now I suppose the drama unfolds in our presence?"

"I didn't expect you to lap this up," Brennan grated, "but I never thought you'd behave like a puberal adolescent. Listen," he said. "Until I came out of Vega's shop none of these things carried much weight as far as I was concerned. I thought perhaps I was a bit nervy as a result of what happened yesterday morning. But in the last hour they've started to jigsaw together —at least, to me they have—and I don't like it. If it was merely a question of a few blasted prints why the hell didn't someone come and ask for copies?"

"Unless I've got the story wrong," Merchant said, "it was you who began the sleight-of-hand. And that 'Mr. Brown' stuff wasn't so smart, either. Santa Martans are as thin-skinned as primadonnas."

"Then why not act accordingly and have a showdown? I'm not in disguise, am I?"

"It's your jigsaw, not mine. Personally, I don't believe it even exists. I'm a coincidence man myself." With practised discretion Merchant glanced towards the other table. "Know him?" he asked Alison.

"Vaguely." She pouted uncertainly. "A week-ender, I think."

"You see?" Merchant scoffed.

Alison turned to Brennan. "Aren't you putting two and two together and making five?"

He didn't answer. A figure plummeted off the top board; water fountained and sloshed.

"Aren't you, Harry?"

"I don't know *what* I'm making. I wish I did."

"Well," Merchant said, showing signs of leaving, "for what it's worth I suggest you finish with the mental arithmetic and concentrate on licking your wounds. Okay—you've had some film ruined and you're mad. Fair enough. But don't, for Pete's sake, start behaving as if you'd got a touch of the sun."

"Is that the best you can do?"

"Here and now, yes."

"Just supposing I'm right, Merchant—just supposing, mind. What would you say then?"

"I never suppose." He rose with a counterfeited smile. "And if I were you I'd stick to your feathered friends—I really would."

"Oh, thanks."

"I mean it, Brennan." Merchant's voice was suddenly a shade

more terse. "Give that imagination of yours a rest. And when you've cooled off you'll probably realise how near you came to sounding plain bloody stupid." He retrieved a cardigan and a couple of cased racquets from behind his chair. "Thanks for the session, Alison. See you—when? Seven tomorrow?"

"Fine," she said.

" 'Bye, then."

They watched him go. Sullenly, Brennan lit another cigarette. He'd expected as much from Merchant. Spoken, his suspicions had had a far-fetched ring, even to himself. Yet they persisted. He couldn't relinquish them. Blowing smoke, he nodded in the direction of the man at the near-by table. "Are you sure about him?"

"Who?"

"Mr. Magazine."

Alison removed her sun-glasses, and her eyes confirmed the set of her lips. "What's gotten into you, Harry? You've been intent on making a mystery out of this right from the start."

He shook his head.

"But you have. And it's ridiculous. You're basing I don't know what on sheer coincidence. Frank's absolutely right."

"Three cheers for Frank. Only it wasn't his film, and it wasn't his room that was searched, and the fellow over there didn't follow him out when he left."

"You're getting wilder all the time—don't you see?" Her hands came into play. "Your room, for instance. Have you got the slightest scrap of proof about that?"

"It was a feeling, I tell you. I woke up to it."

"This morning?"

"Yesterday afternoon—before I took the film to Vega's." He could understand her scepticism; indeed, deep down, he shared it. "Hell, Alison. I normally keep my feet pretty firmly on the ground. I'm as baffled as you are."

"A whole lot more credulous, though. And angry. Small-boy angry."

"I'm angry, all right."

"Well stop it, for God's sake, or I'll follow suit."

It was a side of her he hadn't known before. Merchant's ridicule acted on him like a goad, but Alison's exasperation had the effect of a cold douche. His time with her was rationed and he was allowing himself to be blinkered by an obsession. Chastened, he smiled, endeavouring to suppress the lava-flow of speculation and disquiet; let her move the conversation away to where she wanted it. He had all but forgotten his brusque rejection of Merchant's offer to fix an invitation for him the following night, but she reminded him—not in a manner that harped on his failings, but obliquely, regretting that he wouldn't be present. And if he had been able to segregate one emotion from another he might have realised there and then that he had no cause for jealousy; that she wanted nothing to threaten or diminish the next few days. But he was unable to impose any sort of shape on his mood. Merchant, as usual, had rubbed salt into everything that chafed and frustrated him, and without intent he found his gaze occasionally straying over to the man with the magazine. Whoever he was he was both patient and abstemious; and quite inappropriately dressed to have parked himself at the pool out of choice. It wasn't long before Alison noticed Brennan's continued interest, and though he denied it when she reproved him he was no actor.

"Come on, Harry," she said firmly. "Let's go into lunch. I can't compete out here."

She led him round the pool, a hint of irritation in her quick, short-paced stride. A couple of boys were playing with a beach-ball on the wet mosaic apron, but the pool itself was empty; the blue, transparent water as smooth and glossy as cellophane. After covering about twenty yards Brennan was impelled to look back. Sure enough the man had uncrossed his legs and was rising casually to his feet. Brennan walked on, torn between continuing and turning to bring them face to face. A few paces more and he compromised; bent to attend a shoe-lace. Alison missed him within seconds and stopped to wait. An under-arm glance showed Brennan that the man was approaching: between the pool and the tables the space was confined and he hadn't much option. Brennan transferred attention to his other shoe. Seven or eight yards separated them now, no more, but there was something disconcerting about the indifference with which the gap was being narrowed and Brennan felt a sudden jab of doubt, of foolishness, of having allowed suspicion to over-reach itself. The man was almost level with him as he straightened up. Then everything seemed to happen at once. Without warning the beachball came bouncing past with one of the boys in pursuit. He slipped, cannoning into Brennan, who staggered and grabbed wildly at the passer-by; made contact but failed to hold on. The man grunted, tripped against the pool's raised surround and with flailing arms pitched backwards into the water.

There was a long moment of incredulous silence before he spluttered to the surface. Brennan knelt immediately on the edge, thrusting out a hand, and others joined him, peering over. "I'm sorry," he heard himself repeating. "An accident. It was an accident," but the only answers were gasps and mouth-blown spray. The man clutched the bar and tried to haul himself out, as if doing so would somehow regain him dignity, but his clothes weighed him down and he yielded; accepted all the help on offer. Soon he was standing, soddenly encased, pouring water, bewildered, muttering in Spanish: "My hat. . . . Where is my hat?" Someone plunged in and retrieved it for him, and all the while Brennan was apologising, explaining, offering aid in the shape of a car, a dry-cleaner's—anything that came to mind.

It was a slightly ludicrous scene. "I can't tell you how sorry I am," Brennan insisted yet again. "I tried to save myself when the boy came into me, and—"

"Nobody's fault," the man said, plucking at his clothes. He was middle-aged, quietly spoken and damningly innocuous. "Nobody's fault." He even managed a smile. No, he could manage very well, *gracias*. His car was outside. He had only a short distance to go. No. No, *gracias*. Soon he would be as good as new. Unfortunate, yes, but no one was to blame. . . .

He was quick to recover his poise; absolutely determined that he should be allowed to fend for himself. Brennan went with him as far as the car park, by which time the victim was beginning to steam. A final prod of guilt made Brennan ask for his name and address, but the request was shrugged aside. "That won't be necessary, señor. Not necessary at all."

"You're extremely generous."

There was nothing further to be said or done. Brennan crossed the asphalt to where Alison stood waiting and her mute reception of him was more cold than any words. He was half-anticipating it, though not to such an icy degree. They walked into the Club without speaking and went straight to a table in the dining-room. Once there, she was unable to contain herself any longer.

"It wasn't funny, Harry."

"It was an accident, you know that."

Her dark eyes flashed.

"Hell," he retorted. "Don't be stupid."

"Was waiting for him an accident? Stopping to do your laces? . . . You're worse than any mule, Harry. Why, oh why, can't you leave well alone?"

Something more than mere indignation was driving her. He glimpsed it briefly as it showed itself. At almost any other time he might have made more of it; probed a little, taxed her. But she misled him by adding bitterly: "I work here, Harry. And that kind of thing doesn't do me any good."

CHAPTER SEVEN

Lunch was a polite, strained and joyless forty minutes. Merchant's jibes seemed embarrassingly justified, and Alison's continued coolness was as sobering as it was impenetrable. Though a kind of truce was established and they achieved sporadic exchanges under its flag there were lengthy silences. Time and again a flush of memory or a late-comer's knowing grin highlighted the apparent absurdity of the catalogue of suspicions which anger and Merchant's attitude had forced Brennan to voice. There was, after all, only one solid fact—that he had been deprived of some pictures. The rest was a chain-reaction of conjecture and imagination: more firmly than ever he told himself that it couldn't be anything else. He also told himself that, humbling and unfortunate though the incident was, it had perhaps saved him from some other folly which Alison would have found unforgivable. He was in no position to play a waiting game and he had lost ground with her as it was.

Over the coffee he remembered having dreamt of writing Benedict to explain that he wouldn't be returning as early as planned. Alison had thawed a little by then and he toyed with the idea of telling her. It wasn't the most propitious moment to choose, and he delayed. She was still quietly indignant—and not, he felt, merely because of the business at the pool: there was his obstinacy over Sunday night as well. . . . In the end, he delayed too long. While he slept, the Benedict dream had merged into another; and so it was now—at the very moment he chose to speak. Clouds seemed to break from his mind and with startling vividness he recalled the shadow-play of his conversation with the man in the ceiba tree and the alien, unintelligible replies.

"Yes?" Alison asked.

"I'm sorry. . . ?"

"I thought you were going to say something."

"No," he faltered. "No."

Against his will the question-marks were still there, sharpened with use and hooked in deep, and the sense of disquiet returned like nausea.

Even then he might have managed finally to fight it off if the telephone hadn't buzzed within minutes of his reaching his room. There was nothing he more wanted to do: the last thirty-six hours had been bedevilled enough. He went to the telephone thinking the desk-clerk was probably checking whether he would be in need of a call, but to his astonishment a male voice said: "What d'you speak best after English and Spanish?"

"Who are you?"

"Don't push it for the moment. As sure as eggs are eggs the line's tapped and they'll pull the plug out if it suits them—and quick. . . . What is it? French?"

Brennan hesitated. "German."

"That'll do." It was an eager voice; throaty, not young. "Here goes—*ich spreche deutsch*. That ought to fox them." The sound of indrawn breath rasped along the wire. Then, in halting yet urgent German: "I want us to meet."

"Why? . . . What about?"

"Too difficult to explain. What d'you say?"

"When?"

"Now."

"*Now?*"

"In half an hour. Where they have the cock-fights."

". . . *die hahn kämpfe*": Brennan needed to rack his brains. "I don't know it."

"Near the big cemetery."

"Don't know that either."

"It isn't hard to find. . . . Will you?"

Brennan stalled, on a high-wire of indecision. "Why not here? —at the Oasis?"

"Out of the question."

"You're asking a lot. Give me one good reason."

"Too public." A frustrated groan preceded a relapse into English. "Can you get what I'm aiming at? . . . Manx cat, chum," the voice said cryptically. "Manx cat, I want it."

Brennan frowned. Manx cat? No tail? Understanding rose like a gathering wave. "Got it," he started to say, but the line abruptly went dead and a dribbling sound poured into his ear. He hung up and crossed to the window; looked out on the blazing, somnolent afternoon. Silence, total and persistent, seemed to emphasise his agitation. A full minute elapsed while he warred against the reaction which warned him not to go, not to involve himself. He'd been made a fool of once, and once was enough. Alison was somewhere in his mind but too much was stacked against her and his own resolutions and this time it wasn't imagined. The dream-fragment—yes; but not this sudden and unexpected call or the way in which it had ended. "Manx cat" . . . Brennan felt as if the room were closing in on him. He'd been right after all, then—watched, followed.

Why? . . . Always, it came back to that.

He opened the bureau and rummaged around for a map of La Paz. There were three cemeteries, the largest of which was just beyond the city's western outskirts. The coast road to Monterrey would take him; four miles, say. As he replaced the map he saw the gun in the drawer—an Ortgies automatic which he always packed into his holdall whenever his work led him into the back of beyond. In eight years and a couple of score of countries he had never found a need for it, but its existence was an insurance of sorts. Thoughtfully, he pushed in a magazine and shoved the gun into his hip-pocket. His mind was made up, but he had no illusions. It was no longer any use trying to yield to disbelief. But whether he had found himself an ally or not he could only guess, and he wasn't taking chances.

He used the stairs, thinking, thinking. The entrance-lobby was deserted. Outside, everything stood rooted in its own hard patch of shade and the sky was incandescent. He was watchful, but as far as he could tell only his stunted shadow joined him. He crossed to where he had left the Land-Rover and was forced to use a handkerchief on the door-handle. Under the canvas hood it was stifling. When he pressed the starter-button nothing happened. Cursing, he clambered down and lifted the bonnet, sweat drying almost as fast as it came. He found the solenoid switch and jabbed his finger against the rubber cap, the only remedy he knew; but there wasn't so much as a click. Impatiently, he straightened, and as he did so Alison's harmonica-grilled convertible arrested his gaze. Without a second thought he slammed the bonnet down and strode over. Her ignition-key was in place. He lowered himself into the driving-seat and started up; pulled away with a full-blooded purr. The man on the gate offered a bovine stare but made no attempt to intervene.

At a quarter to three La Paz had the look of a dying city. Scarcely a soul moved on the pavements or lingered at the café tables; only an occasional tramcar sparked along the wires. Brennan had the Avenida del Conquistador practically to himself and at every intersection the lights blinked to indicate a discretionary crossing. As a precaution he left the avenue as soon as he could and took a roundabout route through slums of corrugated tin roofs and plank walls and stinking alleys that no tourist ever saw, then made for the quays. Cheap rooming-houses, sordid bars and fly-blown shops—shuttered now against the torrid heat. Even the craft moored along the sea-wall had all but ceased to rock. He went past *The Conch Shell* and doubled back towards the main east–west thoroughfare as if jolted by a memory. But whatever ruffled Alison—displeasure; anxiety; he still couldn't decide—had lost its restraining hold on him. He had come a long way since last night; even farther since lunch. The pendulum had ceased to swing within a minute of his dropping the receiver on its rest, leaving him rashly determined.

He turned towards Monterrey, tyres whimpering, the empty highway quivering in his rear-view mirror. No one followed, that was certain, but from time to time he checked—no longer as a result of some vague unease, but with matter-of-fact suspicion. He had been stumbling until now. There had been stepping-stones of a kind, but mostly he'd chanced on them, not always thinking they were associated or led anywhere. Only the fiasco at Vega's stuck out, provoking and crucial. Separately, the others were barely sufficient to sustain the weight of distrust. Yet, without them, he wouldn't have been doing what he was—and with a gun in his pocket too.

The telephone conversation smouldered in his mind like a coal. It had been a very English voice. Who was he?—and what did he want? More important, what did he know?

A faded slogan read: SI LÓPEZ SI! La Paz began to lose its solidity as Brennan neared its fringe. The monotony of peeling stucco no longer hemmed him in and the flickering green of banana and mango smallholdings interrupted the implacable glare of reflected sunlight. Dust from the wayside lifted in his wake. Still nothing behind. He passed a pannier-slung convoy of donkeys and a laden cart or two, but little else. The cemetery was somewhere between the road and the sea, and a sign pointed almost as soon as he started looking for one. A dirt track led him from the junction between ragged cactus strips to a walled enclosure and a wide, arched gate. Beyond, as two-dimensional as a back-cloth, Los Colmillos were heaped against the sky, their crumpled confusion softened by haze.

There was no sign of a cock-fight arena. The track continued past the gate. Brennan slowed but went on, looking left and right. La Paz was not quite done with; its waste was apparently dumped here as well as its dead, and a municipal estate crowded the cemetery's seaward limits. A couple of hundred yards beyond the gate the track suddenly widened to form a circular area of bare, flat earth, to one side of which stood a large, open-sided thatched hut—little more than a roof supported on poles. A black saloon was parked near by. A mixture of relief and tension stroked Brennan's nerves when he saw it. He ran the convertible off the track, braking near the other car. It was empty. He glanced round; wondered, hesitated, momentarily apprehensive. As he started to climb out there was movement inside the hut, and a stranger emerged, brushing the thatched overhang.

"Welcome."

Brennan eyed him doubtfully. The voice didn't seem quite the same as on the telephone. The man came towards him, blinking as he extended a hand. He was squat, balding, with an eccentrically-shaped face.

"Mad dogs, eh?" The grip was none too firm. A smile revealed small, discoloured teeth. "The name's Lloyd."

Brennan nodded. Forty? Forty-five? It was difficult to guess.

"Did anyone else try to tag along?"

"If they did I lost them."

"Sure?"

"Absolutely."

"Sorry about that lousy Manx cat pun, but my German's corroded with rust. In the circumstances it's a minor miracle I got you to the right place."

"What's it all about, anyhow?"

"Let's get some shelter, shall we? No point in being baked alive."

They ducked under the thatch. On his guard, Brennan was careful to let Lloyd go first. He seemed harmless enough, but it was too early to be certain. After the glare it was almost dark, but as Brennan's vision adjusted itself he could see half a dozen or more rows of benches set around a worn, board-rimmed patch only a few yards in diameter. The hut had the smell of stale, trapped sweat. There was litter between the benches—used matches, scraps of paper, cheap *cigarro*-butts, empty bottles and broken glass. Lloyd stopped to pick up a blue and bronze feather.

"Have you ever watched a fight?"

"No."

"Then you've been spared. Still, we aren't here to discuss

that—though it's an interesting symbol of the savagery and boredom below the Santa Martan veneer." He tossed the feather away. "Cigarette?"

Brennan took one. As the match flared, he said: "What made you get on to me?"

"Curiosity."

"About what?"

"Ah—now that's complicated. Perhaps I'd better explain who I am?"

"It would help."

"Matthew Lloyd, London *Sunday Herald*." He waited, as if hoping for recognition. Then, with a touch of self-mockery: "Roving reporter. 'Our man on the scene' . . . No? Well, I don't blame you. I make a point of reading a decent paper myself."

Even here the heat was stupefying and the low roof seemed to deaden the resonance of their voices. Brennan straddled a bench and sat down: Lloyd mopped his face. Grim emblems bespattered the cockpit's trampled earth—bloodstains, crusted droppings, smashed and matted quills. It was a foul place, redolent of hate and frenzy.

"Well?" Brennan said.

"Well, credentials over, I saw what happened at the swimming-pool and thought it was high time we got in touch."

"D'you mean to say you've dragged me all the—"

"Hold your horses a moment." Smoke wandered from Lloyd's slightly lopsided mouth. He looked out of condition; constipated. "How long have you known you've been followed?"

"Until you rang I'd only suspected it."

"Any idea why?"

"You tell me. But that fellow at the pool's in the clear. It was an accident."

"Maybe. Frankly, I enjoyed it. Nevertheless, you're wrong about him. He's the one who's dogged you like a second shadow since yesterday evening. Oh yes he has, chum—that very same, very wet gentleman. I can see you're surprised, but surprise doesn't alter the facts. I kid you not . . . Listen," Lloyd went on, "and I'll tell you another thing or two. A plane crashed up in the Colmillos yesterday. You were there. On the way down you

78

stopped off at a bar in Pozoblanco. Then you came to La Paz. . . . Right?"

"You obviously know."

"I only know because I passed through Pozoblanco myself around noon. Quite by chance; I was heading back from Merida. But as luck would have it I chose to sink a couple of beers in the bar you were in earlier. It was full of talk about the crash—pop-eyed, ignorant peasant stuff; useless to me. I thought of going to have a look-see at first-hand, but they made it sound as if I'd need an oxygen mask and God knows what else. Then I heard about you, and I thought: That's my man. Where to find you was the snag. All I'd gleaned in Pozoblanco was that you were a photographer with a Land-Rover—a jeep, they called it; *un heep*." His stained teeth showed. "Well, to cut a long story short, I checked five or six places in La Paz before trying the Oasis. It was about four o'clock by then and the girl on the desk said you were having a zizz until six-ish and weren't to be disturbed. I guessed you were the person I wanted but it seemed a waste of time to hang around so I filled in by making a few routine inquiries about the plane. I drew a solid, cast-iron blank, but there and then it didn't worry me awfully. The name Matthew Lloyd's none too popular in certain quarters—though that's by the way. I got back to the Oasis soon after six with the intention of nabbing you—but someone beat me to it. 'Interpolated himself,' I fancy the phrase should be."

"Meaning?"

"Your reluctant swimmer. He tacked on to you so smartly that I could hardly believe my eyes, but it struck me that if I kept in the background and was patient something might pay off. You went to the post-office, didn't you?"

"Correct."

"Then on to Vega's?"

Brennan nodded.

"So did he—and so did I. Or, to be more accurate, the two of us coffee-shopped around until you came out. Then we all did a motorised Indian file over to the Oasis—after which you and the young lady beat it off to *The Conch Shell*. A. N. Other as well. I gave up at that point, but I found that he was busy doing

79

the rounds with you again this morning—British Embassy, Vega's, and then at the pool . . . To say the least, chum, it's been the kind of devotion that makes an inquisitive bastard like myself put on his thinking-cap. When I rang you I told myself: Careful, if they're all that interested they'll be tapping the line, too—and sure enough they were." Lloyd crushed his cigarette underfoot. "You never cottoned on that it was him, then?"

Brennan shrugged. "Yes and no. I remembered him from breakfast today, but when we'd finished hauling him out of the water I'd given him the benefit of the doubt. He looked so bloody hard done by. Why, I even asked for his name and address."

Lloyd smiled sardonically. "One thing's certain. You'll never see him again. Someone else will take over."

"Charming." Restlessly, Brennan stood up. "You make me sound like a would-be assassin."

"Any theories?"

"Only one that makes an iota of sense."

"The plane?"

"Yes."

"That was my bet, too."

Brennan raised an eyebrow. "What's your interest in this?"

"I want a story, chum. I'll be honest. The *Herald*'s rolling stone has had a long and disastrous losing run, but I've a feeling that—thanks to you and one little item all my own—it might be nearing an end. I'll tell you why in a moment. But first I want to hear your side of things." His breathing wheezed a little. "Did you get any photographs up there yesterday?"

"Yes, but I never saw the results."

"I guessed as much." Lloyd lit another cigarette, hands trembling. "How about going back to the beginning? I find it easier if it comes in sequence, A to Z."

It took Brennan several minutes to piece it all together again, but he welcomed the opportunity if only to clarify his own mind. And it was a relief to unburden himself without incurring scorn. He paced up and down and Lloyd followed him with his eyes, never interrupting, an occasional flicker of his facial muscles denoting suppressed excitement. It was as quiet as in the confessional. An inch-wide trail of ants curled across the floor like a gunpowder fuse. The thatch creaked sometimes, as if there were a weight on it. Beyond its frayed perimeter the clearing shuddered and water-waves of heat jazzed off the two parked cars. Brennan's impression was that he was largely filling in the detail to an outline already shaped and anticipated by Lloyd to meet a professional need. But as for himself he was still in the maze, still groping; able to accept so much and no more.

"What I don't understand," he finished, "is the reason for keeping someone on my heels *after* I'd walked out of Vega's. I don't see the point."

"You could have held back some of your film."

"But I didn't."

"How are they to know? You might not have mailed the rest."

"Then why not haul me in and have done with it?"

"Much too obvious."

Brennan made a defeated gesture.

Lloyd said "Let's see if we can make the penny drop. About the plane. Was it completely burnt out?"

"All except the tail unit."

"Any markings?"

"Not that I remember."

"A hollow blue star, perhaps?"

"I can't say. It was all tangled with lianas, anyhow."

Brennan closed his eyes, focusing the scene, recalling the tail's swept-back leading edges. "It was white."

"Sure of that?"

A nod. "All white."

Lloyd slapped his thighs. "I love you, chum. God, how I love you." He bounced up, scattering ash, employing the now-read-on technique. "Guess whose plane it was."

"Whose?"

"El Presidente's."

"Nonsense."

"I'd wager all I've got and could borrow."

It was Brennan's turn to scoff. "On the strength of its colour?"

"Plus and ace of a whisper I picked up last night."

"You and who else?"

"It was a very exclusive whisper." Lloyd's mouth went sideways as he smiled. "I'd have been happier if you'd seen the star thing, but this is good enough. . . . What did they call it in *El Nuevo Mundo*?—a military transport? . . . Look, two years ago that plane was in the headlines. One gleaming Convair 880 for the President López with love from Washington. A little large something to remember us by. Hands across the sea. Big white dove of peace and friendship."

"Are you suggesting he's been killed?"

"Far from it. I happen to know he's very much alive and kicking."

"What, then?"

"Ah, that's it. Now we've both taken up the slack." Lloyd dropped his cigarette and heeled it in. He sweated profusely. "But here's a President who's lost his outsize runabout through circumstances beyond his control. What happens? Does he announce the fact? No, sir. He puts out a false bit of nonsense in the Press—that took time, incidentally—and privately filches the only pictures of the disaster that exist." He paused; glanced at Brennan. "Don't be under any misapprehension, chum. He runs this island, you know. He really runs it. What López wants, López gets."

"Aren't you forgetting something? At least a couple of dozen people saw the wreck. I wasn't the only one."

"The Pozoblanco lot wouldn't know one aircraft from another. And the others—well, they'd have had their orders. The captain who nailed you was obviously right on the ball."

Unconvinced, Brennan said: "Okay, so it was the President's plane; I won't argue. But what's the purpose of trying to cover up? That kind of property's like a Court elephant. In a week or two at most it's going to be missed—and I don't mean by the Santa Martans. There must be a better reason."

"You're getting warmer."

"Not that I'm aware of."

"Hasn't it occurred to you that the covering up's not so much because of the plane as on account of who was in it? No? . . . Well, it's occurred to me. In fact, it's the only thing that *has* occurred to me." Lloyd paused. "How well d'you know this

82

part of the world?" He didn't wait for an answer, but hurried on: "That fellow up in a tree—the one you photographed."

"Yes?"

"What was he like?"

"Plumpish. Cropped hair."

"A Santa Martan?"

"No."

"European?"

"Saints above, how can I say? How's a European supposed to look, anyway?" Brennan closed his eyes again. The dream was relevant but it seemed preposterous to mention it. A bird flipped through the hut, too fast for identification but checking the flow of his thoughts, making him ask himself what he was doing there; what he hoped to gain. Very rapidly he was getting out of his depth.

"What about the other two?" Lloyd persisted.

"They could have been Eskimos for all I know. Turning the first of them over was enough for me."

"The one in the tree—what sort of complexion?"

"Like zinc. But he was dead, dammit. . . . Hell, Lloyd, what particular will-o'-the-wisp are you chasing? Glorified illegal immigrants?"

"That's a way of putting it."

"In the Presidential plane?" He was beginning to sound like Merchant. "You're letting the *Herald* run away with you."

"Perhaps, perhaps not." Lloyd used the handkerchief as if it were a towel. "Listen, chum. All this hocus-pocus can't be simply because López is afraid to tell Washington he's sorry but their present has been broken and could they please send another. You said as much yourself. An accident's an accident, after all." He licked his lips with a furred tongue. "Don't be fooled by all you see and read. That snug wall-to-wall Pan-Americano stuff—there's less in that than meets the eye for a start. How long have you been here?"

"Three weeks."

"Give me half an hour and I'll complete your education. López knows which side his bread's buttered, but he's on the look-out for jam. That's common knowledge. He's not so fussy

83

where he gets it either. And for what it's worth I reckon the gentleman in the tree and his friends were coming in through the side door with a few samples of what they could offer. It paid off with Castro; why not here?"

Brennan stared, amazement dragging back his scalp.

"Tomorrow," Lloyd continued unabashed, "there's a Palace reception. Yesterday, El Presidente attended Mass at the new basilica. Disarming activities, both of them. Between whiles—what? A hush-hush session with a group of foreign tradesmen up in his mountain retreat. Bring them in one night and send them out the next: no one the wiser. And then what happens? Wham—his personal taxi gets all smashed up and his guests with it. That's bad enough. But to make it worse there's also some character or other who's fluked on the scene with a camera, fooled an officer with a roll of unexposed film and given a false name into the bargain."

"You've got it all worked out, haven't you?"

"I can't see the wind," Lloyd said, "but I can smell what it carries and make a guess where it's been."

Brennan had met Lloyd's breed before—men who, like old-time prospectors, talked of the strike that would surely come if only the luck—and the expenses—held; indestructible optimists who fashioned legends out of rumour and their own imaginations. But never until now had he come across one whose sense of drama so matched his persuasive ability. His mind reeled as Lloyd continued.

"The Russians got into Cuba. What's more they're still there —teeth drawn or no. And they wouldn't turn down an opportunity of getting even a toe-hold in Santa Marta. Dogma eats dogma. It may be small, but this island's volcanic in more ways than one. Graft, corrupt government, Palace revolution and corrupt government again. That's the cycle here." He lit yet another cigarette. "Too far-fetched for you?"

"Too something."

"The cap fits, chum. Washington's tried to keep López sweet as part of United States' Caribbean strategy, but he's an arch schemer with an eye permanently on the main chance. His relations with the States have been on a blackmail basis for quite some time and all the signs are that he's recently been asking too much and too often."

Brennan felt as if he had been presented with an enormous, immovable fact. In the comparatively mild bewilderment of an hour ago he had been uneasy, nettled, convinced that he was under surveillance; peevishly anxious for an explanation. Now, offered one, it was too sensational either to believe or to reject. Yet Lloyd's argument was sufficiently plausible to send a tremor along his spine.

Slowly, he said: "Say, there's a grain of truth in all this, what are you proposing to do?"

"Dig deeper, chum. That's the first thing."

"Then?"

"Get the hell out of Santa Marta and draft the longest cable the *Herald*'s ever received."

"You can't keep it to yourself—not if there's anything in it."

"I can, you know." Lloyd blinked smoke from his eyes. "I've got the legs on everybody else and it's been a long time since that happened. A hell of a time, believe me . . . Listen. I'm groping, groping like mad. All I'm sure about is the plane. I could file a story on the strength of that alone, but I'd have to get out to do it—and I'd never get back in afterwards for the fireworks—if there are any." He looked at Brennan. "Don't get me wrong. When I say I've got the legs on everybody I'm not necessarily including the Embassy boys. The news-pack, yes; but not them. They don't miss very much in those ivory towers of theirs."

"You wouldn't say that if you'd been with me before lunch."

Lloyd didn't seem to hear. "My Boy Scout days are over, chum. I've been gagged before. Things can keep for a bit yet." He glanced at his watch. "I tell you what. It's three thirty. How about coming up to Pozoblanco for a snoop around? The day's still young."

"You won't discover anything there."

"Why not? It's near enough to the scene of the crime." Lloyd grinned mirthlessly, stranger to stranger. "And we can always pick each other's brains on the way."

Brennan hesitated, not least because of Alison's car. It would be dark before they returned to La Paz. Already he had learned

85

enough to convince her that he hadn't been off his head; enough to make Merchant eat his words. And yet . . .

"Come on," Lloyd was urging. "You're in this up to your neck as it is. Wouldn't it be nice to know exactly why?"

CHAPTER EIGHT

LLOYD had no objection to leaving his saloon to fry in the sun. As he settled into the convertible beside Brennan he remarked: "Bright of you to borrow the lady's."

"I didn't. I just took it."

"Oh, oh."

Dust curdled in their wake as Brennan put his foot down. They were on the road within minutes, heading west through fields of black soil and tamed plantation-vistas, the hills rising ahead.

"By the way," Lloyd said. "Odd to mention it now, I suppose, but—well, glad to know you. When your name clicked with me yesterday I thought: Ah, now there's a real pro. He'll understand what I'm after."

"I'm a flaming amateur, make no mistake. Things like this happen to other people."

The last of the wayside hoardings fell behind. The rushing air was heavy with the sweet, hot smell of the land and Brennan lifted his face to it like a man coming home. Almost always, no matter where he found himself, he experienced a sense of release when he left a city, any city; a renewal of wonder and elemental joy, order after chaos. But not this time. His mind was in upheaval and he drove fast, unrelaxed, weighing Lloyd's devastating hunches, one part of him wanting to go on, another anxious to wash his hands of it all and turn back. As the miles committed him he felt increasingly guilty about the car and with the best will in the world he couldn't see what Lloyd hoped to unearth in Pozoblanco.

At one point he voiced his misgivings. "If you're thinking of doing any climbing you can tackle it alone." He was blunt. "Half an hour in Pozoblanco and I'm heading for La Paz."

"I thought I might nab the priest Johnny and that sergeant of police."

"I can't see them giving you any sort of lead."

"Great oaks from little acorns grow." The *Herald*'s style was never far away.

The road was beginning to rise a little. On either side the forest flowed off the slopes on to the edges of the plain like the tip of a vast green glacier. Carrion crows got up, clap-clap-clap, cawing indignantly. Ahead, the looping route over the escarpment showed like a trail of brown string.

Presently, shifting position, Lloyd said a curious and revealing thing: "Does the Imjin ring a bell with you?"

"The what?"

"The Imjin. Imjin River . . . Korea."

"Vaguely." Brennan shot him a baffled glance. "What's the connection?"

"I am, chum." Lloyd's twisted smile was self-conscious. "I won't bore you with the fusty details, but that was my finest hour. For a lot of poor sods it was their last, but for Matthew Lloyd it meant belated elevation to the front page. The *Herald*'s glory boy was born by accident on the Imjin a decade and more ago, since when his career hasn't exactly fulfilled the high hopes of those who loyally continue to employ him. My kind of person's as good as his last story, maybe his last but one—you'll know how it is. And for the past few years I seem to have been going off at half-cock or failing to go off at all. What do you suppose happened at Suez? Fever—on the day of the landings. I covered the whole affair from a cruiser's sick-bay, which is fine if you're a strategist but no damn good if you're meant to be doing the intrepid impressions. Hungary was much the same: I never got nearer than Vienna. Cyprus—don't talk to me about Cyprus. Or Katanga. God; wrong-place-at-the-wrong-time Lloyd, that was me." He broke off as Brennan swerved to avoid a pothole. "There's a limit to what you can cook up, chum, and getting older doesn't help when it comes to the close-quarters stuff. I'm forty-seven, and there are days when I feel about as solid as a sieve. I need this story more than any ageing spinster ever needed a man, but desperation isn't the best of substitutes for whatever's gone. Sometimes I reckon I left the best part of that commodity on the Imjin." He was silent, then added: "I suppose what I'm trying to say is that it gets harder."

He was as confiding as a lonely drinker in a bar, yet far from maudlin. A trifle hunched, wispy hair streaming, he even managed a certain dignity. The gun pressing into Brennan's rump was a reminder that he had invested him with dangerous potentialities, and to have done so wasn't as ludicrous as it might have now seemed. There was something alarming about Lloyd's admission, particularly since he was so clearly determined to make the facts fit the pattern he had summarily allotted them.

"*This* story" . . . Brennan eyed him cautiously, discovering a person gone soft at the core yet driven by necessity; a perilous combination.

"If you're right about it being the President's plane," he said, "you've got a story already."

"I'm right, all right."

"Well, let me get out of Santa Marta before you use it, that's all I ask."

"You don't go along with the López *volte-face* idea?"

"There could be other explanations."

"Give me a 'for instance'."

"That's your line of country, not mine. But, for God's sake, don't shut your mind to the possibility that you may be wrong. I want to leave this island in one piece."

"You will, chum. Never fear." They were through the village at the base of the escarpment now. Ragged children scrabbled in the dirt. "Sometimes," Lloyd said, "a volcano splutters along for years before it really blows. Since the Cuba affair died a death I've been hanging about the Caribbean wondering where and when the next eruption would be. López is a wily operator with his hand in the till. Washington's fed and clothed him up to the hilt, but he's a free agent and I wouldn't put it past him to have done what I think he has."

"You've got damn-all to go on."

"I've got what's happened to you and your pictures and that's a good enough lynch-pin."

He was beginning to be a discomfiting ally. It was one thing for Brennan to have wanted his own nagging suspicions confirmed; quite another to find himself the very mainspring of Lloyd's headline ambitions. All very well to be told: "In for a penny, in for a pound, eh?"—but it simply wasn't so. He hadn't asked to be 'in' anything and there was nothing to be gained by wading deeper. That sort of water was for those who could swim and Lloyd's compulsion towards it—eager and nervous at the same time—was a little frightening. As far as Brennan was concerned Santa Marta meant humming-birds, bold and beautiful hills rising out of the sea, orchids and bougainvillaea and crested palms, swarthy skins and climbing orchids, rum and maraccas and molten sunsets. If—as Cooper had said at the Embassy that morning—the fruit was rotten under the skin, he could only bow to local knowledge. Poverty, ignorance, inequality, disease—he wasn't blind, but pity without power was as useless as time without hope. He did his work and moved on. Political machinations weren't his concern. Chance had flicked a wing at him yesterday, and Lloyd had given substance to his subsequent uneasiness; proved him right. Minor mysteries remained, but the over-riding Why? that Lloyd now pursued was ceasing to be an obsession. Every time he thought of Alison he did so with an increasing twinge of disquiet. Whatever hasty notion had started him on this particular journey had lost its impetus and he could imagine nothing better—or wiser—than being in his room at the Oasis and sweating through an afternoon's sleep. It was already after four: he couldn't hope to reach La Paz before seven.

To hell with López and Lloyd's wishful thinking. Alison mattered; no one else . . . Whereas Lloyd was saying: "If only I could lay my hands on those pictures of yours. That would really put the cat among the bloody pigeons."

Brennan negotiated the escarpment as fast as he dared, sounding the horn almost continuously, swinging wide on the coiling turns. The plain flattened out behind, the lavender distances blurred, El Conquistador's crumbling citadel no larger than a toy fort on a garbage mound. The air streamed like silk over their damp skins. Half-way up they squeezed past a shuddering, downward-bound truck, but there was no other traffic and the nippy convertible made short work of the gradients. Neither spoke for some time, Brennan because he was fully occupied. Only when the escarpment was finally done with and the road's demands were mild by comparison did Lloyd come out of his thoughtful shell.

"What sort of fellow was the police-sergeant?"

"Pompous. The military very soon put him in his place."

"A talker?"

"Oh yes."

"A lot of them aren't. They just stare like snakes. What about the priest?"

"I didn't have much to do with him."

"They're brighter than most as a rule."

With irritation, Brennan said: "Just what d'you hope to learn?"

"God knows, chum. Maybe we'll draw a blank. But at least—"

" 'We'? . . . Now, listen. I'm in this only so far as I've found myself in it. Let's get that clear. I've told you all I can and you've confirmed what I suspected was going on. That more or less satisfies me."

"But you're still involved."

Brennan shrugged.

"When you pitched your well-dressed shadow into the swimming-pool you probably gave yourself a few hours' grace. But they're unlikely to have lost interest. You'll find they'll slap someone else on as soon as you get back. Unless I miss my guess they're in a quandary about you. They've blocked your photographs, but they aren't sure what's remained up here." Lloyd tapped his forehead. "And they daren't get you out of the country on a trumped-up charge in case you turn nasty and start remembering things. So they go on keeping an eye on you and the company you keep. Hell, chum, you're involved—like it or not. You can't opt out."

"I needn't dig any deeper, though."

"Other fish to fry, eh?"

"Meaning?"

Lloyd smiled his off-centre smile. "The young lady."

There was a slight pause before Brennan answered. If he was involved, then so was Alison and whatever the next few days might build for them. The enormity of Lloyd's assumptions about López and his hunger for evidence endangered others besides himself. If he probed too obviously, miscalculated, over-reached, trouble could ricochet in all directions. A warning was called for, and Brennan said: "You might not be the only one who gets hurt."

Lloyd's mouth twitched, but he made no response. The forest pressed in on them, echoing the engine's beat. They passed a woman plodding knock-kneed under a huge load of cut wood; some men at work on a culvert. Parakeets scattered with a kaleidoscopic flutter of scarlet and green. A waterfall showed in a purple ravine like a silver scar. For another mile the road bucked and squirmed to no apparent purpose: then, after only a warning glimpse or two, Pozoblanco suddenly began—shacks and cactus-fenced huts that gradually gave way to the shabby solidity of double-storeyed façades and the central plaza with its broken fountain. To Brennan, it seemed that an enormous length of time had elapsed since he was last there. The place looked even smaller than he remembered it; some of it even more wretched. He steered for the blunt oblong of shade thrown by the church and he and Lloyd climbed stiffly out on to the cobbles. The afternoon's lethargy was ending. A few stalls doing business near the court-house, melons being unloaded from a cart, gaunt lounger seeking the solace of an early rum.

Misgivings swept Brennan again as he and Lloyd headed for the police-station. "What in the hell are you going to ask?"

"Not," Lloyd retorted, "whether anyone remembers a hollow blue star, so don't panic." His glance was unfriendly. "Perhaps you'd rather not come in?"

"On the contrary. Perhaps I'd better."

A policeman squatted on a stool just inside the doorway. He stood up as they passed, rifle-butt scraping on worn tiles. Doors opened off a corridor beyond a varnished wooden barrier. A clock with only one hand, a crinkled portrait-print of El Presidente, a pair of oil lamps bracketed to the wall and a cheap brass bell screwed to a pillar. The effect was monastic; the atmosphere venal. Lloyd pinged the bell, but no one came. The man at the door watched with interest, then decided he perhaps ought to do something.

"Yes?" he said, sloping nearer.

"Is the sergeant available?" This was Lloyd.

"No."

"Who is, then?"

"The clerk only."

"Where is everybody?"

"Out or off duty."

"Where's 'out'?"

"On the road."

Lloyd grunted. To Brennan he said: "Was he one of yesterday's bunch?"

"No."

The policeman seemed tongue-tied except when confronted with a question. He shifted his feet, waiting for the next. Thickset, a peasant's face, slow-witted eyes—he was far from promising material, and to Brennan's relief Lloyd accepted the fact. Looking round, he said casually: "Where is this place?"

"Pozoblanco, señor."

"Pozoblanco." Lloyd made a show of ignorance. "How far is Merida?"

"Forty kilometres."

"Which way?"

"Left out of the plaza, then straight on. *Todo seguido.*"

"*Gracias.*" Lloyd nodded, and Brennan followed him into the glare. Music sounded from an adjacent saloon. Alison's dusty convertible looked memorably conspicuous and more than ever Brennan regretted having come. If this was a sample of Lloyd's method it wasn't encouraging.

"Look," he said. "No one's been sitting on *your* tail and that isn't *your* car. Keep it in mind, will you?"

"Cold feet?"

"I don't see how you can pump anybody without arousing suspicion."

Lloyd jerked a thumb. "That one's as harmless as a new-born lamb. And don't forget—they believe what they read in *El Nuevo Mundo*. If they can read at all, that is."

"Are you going to try the priest?"

"I am indeed. But in case our policeman-friend is watching I think it would be as well if we had a gape at the church."

The bleached, iron-studded doors were shut, but they yielded easily enough. The gloom of the gilded interior was pierced by angled shafts of sunlight: the still air reeked of damp and sour incense. Automatically, Brennan crossed himself. A couple of women were washing the sanctuary floor and one of them, as dark and wrinkled as a raisin, offered to fetch the priest.

Brennan said: "You can't ask him the way, too."

"We can admire his church, though."

"He'll remember me. He's bound to."

"A few pesos as a thank-offering will interest him more. Anyway, it's so dark in here—"

"It's a risk."

"By the same token it was a risk going into the police-station."

"I know. And I'm damned glad the sergeant wasn't there." The effect of Lloyd's gesture was inflammatory. "*I'm* not trying to prove anything," Brennan snapped, his meaning double-edged. "*C'est magnifique*, and all that, *mais ce n'est pas la guerre*."

He turned and walked down the aisle, leaving Lloyd standing. A twisted white body of the crucified Christ pierced the unnatural dusk. He pushed through the door and went to the car. Some children gathered, a few to stare, others to beg. He couldn't for the life of him understand what scraps of information Lloyd expected to prise out of the old priest and he felt exposed by having to wait in the plaza. The last thing he wanted was to draw attention to himself and the car by creating a scene. He parted with all his small coins; sat and suffered while the bolder children finger-scrawled in the dust on boot and bonnet.

He had lied to Lloyd: the *Herald*'s faded glory boy could go hang if need be. As the minutes passed he was conscious of a sneaking respect for the sanity of Merchant's scepticism. But whereas Merchant hadn't believed a word he had said, it was difficult not to believe Lloyd—at least in so far as it having been the President's plane. And once the plane's identity was accepted, more momentous explanations were called for; he couldn't shake the logic of *that*. Lloyd's was sensational in the extreme, but the possibility of his being even near the mark was enough to demand the utmost caution. Instead of which . . .

Angrily, Brennan shielded the horn-button to prevent a grinning child from getting at it. Come on, his mind urged. Come *on* . . . The jagged graph-line of the Colmillos ridges showed above the court-house roof and he fretted, thoughts turning more and more towards Alison, all too well aware of the irony that in an endeavour to justify himself he was exposing her to whatever repercussions Lloyd's hell-bent neurosis might bring about. Here he was, in her car—without so much as a by-your-leave, either—dabbling crudely in something best left to those whose business it was: and by that he didn't mean Lloyd. He could hardly complain if she found his action irresponsible, unpardonable, even.

A quarter of an hour dragged by before Lloyd emerged from the church. He walked with a springing gait that to Brennan seemed forced, in conscious defiance of middle age. On the other hand the sun caused him to squeeze his eyes and the facial creases were unkind, making him look older than he was. But the eyes themselves were as eager as if he had just downed a couple of bracing drinks.

"Well?"

"Something attempted, something done." Lloyd slammed the car door after him. The children edged away. "He's as shortsighted as a bat. He wouldn't have known you from Adam any more than he could describe the plane."

"He mentioned it, then."

"Oh, yes—without prompting, either. In fact he was full of it. He said a Mass for the dead this morning. Requiem Mass—is that what you call it?" Not much escaped him.

"Yes."

"There were fifteen killed apparently. But listen to this. He implied that Mass was offered on spec, as it were, for all fifteen. Like any ignorant Protestant I asked what he meant and he told me that he never saw any bodies. He said they were all burned in the fire. *All* of them, chum, *all of them*."

"Where'd he get that idea?"

"From the captain. When he first arrived on the hillside the captain passed him on to a lieutenant."

"That's right," Brennan nodded. "But before we started the climb I mentioned both to him and the police-sergeant that I'd come across three bodies."

"Exactly. He asked the lieutenant where they were and the lieutenant replied that he didn't know what he was talking about. Then the captain rejoined them. The priest repeated his question and the captain said at once—*muy pronto*—that he had been misinformed; that everyone in the fuselage had gone for a Burton."

"And he believed it?"

"Obviously. I couldn't press him, mind." Lloyd fumbled for cigarettes. "Curiouser and curiouser, eh? It all ties together nicely."

"What else did you get?"

"Nothing. But this is as good as I'd hoped for. What's more, it'll look well in print. No stone unturned." Lloyd lit up with an air of triumph. "I was very discreet, don't worry."

Brennan switched on. The more Lloyd's theory gained support the more anxious he was to be going.

"Just one more thing, chum. One last thing."

"What?"

"Take the Merida road for a mile or two."

"For God's sake!"

"Only a mile or two. Partly to please the law"—Lloyd gestured towards the police-station—"and partly to let yours truly have a gander at the hill in question. Just to have had it in my sights—you know? . . . It's a small, private feeling."

With bad grace Brennan swung the way Lloyd asked, accelerating out of the village. It had gone five and shadows were beginning to sprout across the land. Labourers moved in the fields and on the terraced slopes. Creamy fists of cumulus were clenched along the western skyline, awaiting the sun.

'Only a mile or two,' Lloyd repeated.

Los Colmillos changed position as the road snaked. A blue jay screamed from a pepper tree. Lloyd peered at the succession of false crests obscuring the main ridge. Another couple of minutes ought to satisfy him, Brennan thought. After that—*finis*. Once they were back at the cock-fight arena Lloyd could go his own way; find and fend for himself. He was on to something—there wasn't much doubt about it. But from now on the stepping-stones were all his. . . .

And then, as they topped a slight rise, he saw a couple of soldiers on the crown of the camber. With a spasm of alarm he obeyed their signal and brought the convertible whimpering to a halt. The following wave of dust sifted over the soldiers, one of whom, carbine slung, coughed and turned away to spit.

The other said: "No stopping for ten kilometres, señor."

"Oh?"

He was affable enough, but businesslike. "Ten kilometres, understand?"

"Why?"

"Orders."

He was about to motion them on, but his companion asked: "What's your destination?"

Lloyd was very quick. "La Paz."

"La Paz? But that's the other way."

"Surely not? In the village just now—"

"The other way, señor."

Lloyd spread his hands like a man bemused; glanced at Brennan. "About turn, chum . . . *Gracias, amigos*. Imagine what my wife would have said if the ship had sailed without me."

He was a good liar: the soldiers laughed. As Brennan worked the wheel on a three-point turn one of them said admiringly: "Fine car. *Magnifico*. Yours?"

Brennan avoided answering, but the soldier persisted.

"Yours, señor?"

He nodded grudgingly, like someone found out. The near-side wheels bumped on the verge as he completed the turn and started to pull away.

"*Adios*," Lloyd called over his shoulder, very much the tourist still. But his expression changed when Brennan spoke.

"They've taken the number."

"Nuts."

"They have. I can see them in the mirror. One of them's got his notebook out."

Hell, he thought. Bloody hell . . . Misgivings cascaded over him. He hated Lloyd suddenly, hated himself, hated the whole blasted, stinking, wretched business. He careered through Pozoblanco as if it weren't there, deaf to Lloyd's argument that the man might have been reaching for a cigarette-pack, a wallet, a comb . . . anything; convinced he wasn't mistaken.

"Not to worry," Lloyd reasoned, pouring oil. "I ask you— why in the blazes should they want your number?"

"It's not *my* number, as you damn well know."

Brennan drove on, his meaning clear, his thoughts aflame. For a long time he spoke no more and Lloyd was also silent. For mile after twisting mile they kept themselves to themselves. Five thirty, five forty-five, six o'clock . . . La Paz had never seemed so far. By the time they reached the escarpment the tropical dusk was beginning to form—the swollen sun dipping fast over the sweltering plain, the air losing its clarity. "Easy," Lloyd protested as the tyres snickered near the edge, but Brennan had done with listening to him. *You* sweat, he thought. Earlier, he might have been persuaded not to disclose what had happened that afternoon. ("A head start, chum. That's all I want. . . .") Not now, though. The carrot Lloyd was reaching for was too dangerous. Alison would have to be told. If there was the slightest chance of her being drawn into a game of blind-man's buff she had a right to know. And there was a chance. Even if she hadn't missed the convertible by the time he got back he was going to tell her where he'd taken it, and why. . . .

Lamps in the village at the escarpment's base; the smell of wood-smoke mixed with ordure. A purple stain thickening over the plantations. The first bats. Headlights on. Evening traffic on the road towards Monterrey hump-backed cattle like dark statues near the wayside. Six thirty, and still about nine miles to go: five or so to the cock-fight hut by the cemetery. Green rays flickered beautifully through layers of burning cloud as the sun's rim finally vanished into the sea, but for once Brennan didn't cock an ear in child-like fancy for the giant extinguishing hiss that never came.

Lloyd at last regained contact between them. "Here, have this." He pushed a card into Brennan's top pocket.

"You needn't have bothered."

"Something might come up. You never know."

Brennan shook his head.

"Hear no evil, see no evil? . . . Well, I wish you joy. Thanks for your help, anyway. And good luck. But watch out. They may find an excuse to nail you yet." The track to the cemetery was showing in the beam of the lights, and he said: "This'll do. I'll walk down. As if I hadn't guessed, you're in a hurry." Lloyd opened the door and got out, finger-combing what hair there was. The tree-frogs were in full voice. "By the way—if you happen to bump into me publicly, forget we ever met. I will. The chances are Big Brother will be watching, and I've plenty of ferreting still to do."

"Aren't you satisfied?"

"I'll be satisfied when I know who they were, chum. *Exactly* who they were . . . Every picture tells a story." Lloyd's weak, lopsided smile was just discernible. "Well, *adios*. Read all about it, eh?"

The night erased him. Ahead, the diffused pink glow of La Paz brightened the sky. It was twelve minutes to seven as Brennan pierced the city's fringes. He had thought so much and for so long since leaving Pozoblanco that nothing new cluttered his mind. It was no use blaming Lloyd—no use blaming anyone but himself. The clocks were pointing to the hour when he passed the floodlit Palace. Just how gullible had he become? It was strange to be sure of so little yet apprehensive of so much. The traffic-lights were with him all the way down Conquistador. Seconds after wheeling round the glittering fountain at its end he was moving through the Oasis's gates, and the very normality of the place seemed to brand as a lie everything Lloyd had suggested. Yet disbelief had gone for good.

He ran the convertible over to where he had taken it from, wondering if he were already being watched again, whether Alison had missed it, how and where he should start to explain. His head buzzed with the continuing sensation of movement and he didn't immediately realise that the peremptory voice he heard was addressing him.

"Huh?" Turning wearily, he saw the gate-warden and a white-helmeted municipal policeman.

"*Buenas tardes*," white helmet was saying—echoing the soldier at Pozoblanco; another policeman earlier in the day. "Your car?"

Brennan's heart sank. "No."

"You admit that?"

"Of course. I borrowed it."

"Name?"

"Brennan."

"This car has been reported stolen." The policeman muttered something to the attendant, who nodded.

"I think there must be some misunderstanding," Brennan said, a reason dawning. "The owner and I know each other. She won't object to my having used it."

"You had permission?"

"No." Brennan emphasised the denial. "The lady hadn't the least idea I had taken it or where I was going. But my own vehicle had broken down and—"

"The charge is stealing, señor."

"*Charge?* Hell, the thing's back, isn't it?"

The policeman lifted his shoulders. "The charge remains."

"What's the fine?"

"That will be for the magistrate to decide."

Brennan smothered his indignation. "Who instigated this? . . . You?" he fired at the attendant.

"No," white helmet cut in. "The lady concerned."

"Is she in the Club?"

"It is possible."

"Well, if you'd ask her to step outside you'll find there's been

99

a mistake. When she missed the car she naturally imagined it had been stolen. Ask her to be good enough to step outside for a moment, will you?"

"Very well."

Another muttered exchange and the attendant went away, disappearing into the brightly-lit entrance. A dyspeptic rumble of traffic reached them; the buzz of conversation from the bar. Someone in a tuxedo passed, pretending he wasn't interested.

Looking the car over, the policeman asked: "Where did you take it, señor?"

"Nowhere special."

"It was dusty, wherever it was."

Brennan noticed DOLORES scrawled across the boot; PLAZA DE LA FUENTE, mis-spelt. He smeared the words through with the flat of his hand, wondering what else the children in Pozoblanco had written. "Dusty's right." He tried to smile, heart thumping a little. It seemed a long time before Alison emerged and started down the steps. He walked towards her, sure of himself, uneasy only about what he must tell her after the policeman had gone.

"Sorry to drag you out, Alison, but there's a bit of a storm in a teacup brewing here. Believe it or not, I'm being accused of pinching your car." Her back was towards the light and he couldn't see her face properly. "Could you tell them it's all a mistake? I'll explain later."

The policeman intervened. "Do you wish to press your charge, señorita?"

To Brennan's utter amazement she nodded.

"Alison!"

"Is this the man?"

She wouldn't look at him. Stunned, he listened to her say: "Yes, *guardia*. This is the man."

CHAPTER NINE

In the back of a urine-stinking wagon the policeman offered Brennan a cigarette. "They are unpredictable, eh, señor? The more you know them, the less you know them." He grinned, enjoying the experience of escorting a foreigner who was other than a drunken *marinero*. "Now you wonder. Now you scratch your head." He, too, was a man of the world.

Brennan sat in a daze, Alison's words ringing in his ears. The wagon rattled along a dream of murky streets. Even now he couldn't believe it had happened. "This is the man"—at which she had swung on her heels and walked back into the Club and white-helmet had touched him on the arm: "This way, señor". . . . Why? In God's name, why? He felt almost sick. Just because he had borrowed her car?

He leaned against the metal side of the wagon, beyond reasoning, beyond trying to seize the chance of buying the policeman off. They travelled for only a few minutes, but in which direction Brennan neither knew nor cared. He couldn't seem to unclench his fist or unknot his jaws. When the wagon stopped the flap was let down and he got out. The policeman attempted to take him by the arm, but he shook the hand away, anger beginning to smart. There were double doors into a building, a badly-lit lobby with a wooden barrier like the one in Pozoblanco, a desk with a smarmed-hair individual holding a fly-swat.

"Name?"

"Brennan." He was beginning to think there had never been a time when he hadn't been confronted by sullen men in creased uniforms.

"Full name?"

"Harry Sean Brennan." Spell *that*, he thought savagely.

"Nationality?"

"Irish."

"Occupation?"

"Photographer."

"And the offence?" A glance at the escort.

"Theft," the policeman said. "He stole a lady's car."

The way had narrowed down to this, then. Theft. "Yes, I press the charge." . . . Brennan closed his eyes like someone betrayed.

"Turn out your pockets."

He obeyed insolently. Cigarettes, Ronson lighter, Waterman pen, nail-clipper, handkerchief, leather wallet containing forty-four SM dollars, eighteen pesos in loose change, one Ortgies 7·65-calibre automatic. He produced the loaded gun last, placing it amongst the other things, not tossing it down like the rest.

"What else?"

"Nothing."

The man at the desk took his word for it, as if the surrender of a gun implied total capitulation. He picked up the automatic and studied it with interest. Head tilted sideways, he asked: "Have you a licence?"

"No."

"Why do you carry a weapon like this?"

"For self-protection."

"Against whom?"

"Twenty thousand armed police for a start."

"In the circumstances I suggest that is a bad joke."

"It wasn't a joke." Anger was welling up, reaching out in baffled protest. "I want," Brennan said, "to speak with somebody from my Embassy."

"Later."

"The British Embassy acts on behalf of Irish nationals. There's a Mr. Charles Cooper—"

"Later. First I require a statement about this car."

"It belongs to a Señora Stacey at the Oasis Club," white-helmet said. "According to the *conserje* it was driven away between two thirty and three o'clock this afternoon."

"By the accused?"

"Yes."

"Where is it now?"

"At the Club. It was returned a little after seven."

"By the accused?"

"Yes."

The man at the desk finished scratching his notes. "You admit this?" he asked Brennan.

The telephone buzzed.

"Wait, please."

There was a bench against the wall and Brennan moved to it, shattered and resentful. "The accused". . . . A hundred-kilometre drive, a suspicion proved, a fantastic hunch partially authenticated, a growing sense of guilt for having possibly implicated Alison—and now this. It was inexplicable; humiliating. He couldn't even begin to understand what had possessed her. Her face had been shadowed; her voice low. And she had turned her back on him as soon as possible, as if he were a stranger. Pique? She wasn't that small, surely?

He couldn't hear what was being said into the telephone: in any case it seemed unlikely to concern him. He sat woodenly, trying to resurrect his wits, fumbling for a clue to account for Alison's behaviour. Everything was going too fast for him, but he didn't have long in which to come to terms with it. After a couple of minutes he was called over to the desk again. He was met with a hard, embattled look.

"There are other questions."

"Such as?"

"Not from me. The *jefe* will see you."

"The *jefe*?" Brennan felt a prick of alarm. His tone was guarded. "Look, if there's to be a song and dance about this . . . this farce, I insist on your contacting the British Embassy right away."

"Headquarters will attend to that. My instructions are that you are to be taken down there at once."

Brennan's thoughts were beginning to race. The dominant image in his mind was of the soldiers at Pozoblanco noting the convertible's number: not for the first time he seemed to be getting his proofs too late. But there were others, confused, whirled away like blown leaves. And there was Lloyd's "They're in a quandary about you"; Alison's "Why, oh why can't you leave well alone?"

"I shall want those things of mine back."

"You will be given a receipt."

"I've heard that one before."

He looked for any sign of misunderstanding, anything to show that there was more to this than the result of pettiness over a borrowed car. But in vain. Yet the phone-call had been to do with him, that was obvious. Alison would know where he was and Lloyd knew where he had been. But, significantly, someone knew both. As the receipt was made out he said carefully: "What's so wrong about driving to Marbon, can you tell me that?" But he drew no more than a shrug. What would a clerk have to divulge, anyway? . . . He took the proffered receipt, and as he pushed it down into his top pocket his fingers touched the card Lloyd had given him. There and then he was conscious of making no decision, but the feel of it lingered, stoking his pulse-rate. The escort accompanied him out to the wagon and pulled up the flap behind them; thumped on the back of the driver's cabin. They lurched away with a crash of gears, honking into the traffic's stream.

Police headquarters was close to the Avenida del Conquistador, but to begin with Brennan did not recognise where he was. It wounded him even to think of Alison. The last half-hour had made havoc of the rest of his stay in Santa Marta. He couldn't fathom her motives, but whatever they were they had thrown a net over him. As recently as yesterday she had been saying: "You're a long way from home, Harry. You don't want trouble. . . ." The line of his lips hardened as the irony burned deeper. The so-called theft of a car and the unlicensed possession of a gun camouflaged whatever awaited him at headquarters. A chief of police would hardly demean himself by handling two-a-penny charges like that. "Something to nail you with, chum. . . ." Lloyd seemed right again, in this as in so much else. Now they could put him into cold storage for a while; tactfully prevent any more meddling. *They*. And to think that Alison, of all people, had plonked the opportunity into their lap. . . .

The wagon was nearing Conquistador. His escort rubbed the pressure-weal caused by the helmet, lulled by Brennan's passivity, relishing a few minutes of unbuttoned relaxation. The tension in Brennan was mounting. Unwittingly, Alison had saved herself from being compromised; but Lloyd was somewhere at large. If the stakes were as high as he made them out to be, one question too many, one false contact, and he would smell the inside of a police-wagon, too. It no longer seemed fantastic to Brennan that he had almost come round to accepting his point of view. With the powerlessness of a swimmer he felt himself in the grip of a sinister undertow—and sinking deeper all the time. But it was against Alison that his fists were clenched. If she had deserved better of him, then so had he of her.

They rattled into the palm-lined avenue. It was thronged, strident, gaudy with neon. At an intersection half-way along they were halted by the lights and drew abreast a coach-load of tourists. It gave Brennan an extraordinary sensation to see them, safe and secure in their glass cocoon, and the thought of their ignorance caused him a moment's impotent envy. Once inside police headquarters there wasn't much he could do except insist on his right to see Charles Cooper. The prospect of kicking his heels in some cell or other with nothing but bewilderment for company acted on him like a spur. More than anything he wanted to shake Alison by the shoulders and force a reason out of her; make her look him in the face.

His fingers touched Lloyd's card again. They were turning out of the avenue. White-helmet struck a match and cupped his hands to a half-smoked cigarette, concentrating as the driver braked. Without warning there was a loud explosion and the wagon lurched and seemed to shake itself. Then it slowed, the floor tilting, the blown tyre flapping. The two of them picked themselves up from the floor and blinked at one another. "*Caramba!*" Curses sounded from the front and the driver's door opened and slammed. The escort recovered his helmet and rammed it on; hurriedly let the flaps down and got out. Hands on hips he and his compatriot stared at the damage, engrossed, vociferous. The inevitable crowd began to gather and Brennan suddenly realised that his presence was temporarily forgotten.

He didn't give himself time to think. Quietly, inconspicuously, he dropped into the road and began to walk, slowly at first, then more quickly. Then he put his head down and started to run.

He had a fifty-yard start before the shouting began. Unencumbered by heavy boots and restricting accoutrements he rapidly widened the gap between himself and his pursuers, sprinting for all he was worth, dodging cars, side-stepping gaping pedestrians. He seemed to bring passers-by to a standstill only as he drew level with them. Behind, a whistle blew repeatedly. Someone more quick-witted than most made a half-hearted attempt to bar his way, but Brennan shoved him aside and careered on, left into a side street, then right, then left again, abandoned to the thought of getting clear. Once the opportunity had presented itself and the impulse took him there was no stopping; no going back.

Gradually, the sounds of pursuit diminished. He slowed his pace so as not to attract attention and looked less often over his shoulder. Before long he was able to walk again; mingle discreetly. When he was perhaps a quarter of a mile and a score of ill-lit turnings from where he had quit the wagon he took refuge in a bar. It was a noisy, crowded place, fogged with smoke. Clerks came here; shopkeepers, petty officials. There were no uniforms. Breathless, Brennan stood at the counter and watched the bead-curtained entrance. He had no notion of what he was going to do or where he would make for next. Only now, when approached by the bartender, did he realise just how vulnerable he was. He hadn't parted with his watch, but, otherwise he was as good as naked. "No," he said. "Nothing"— and for the moment the man was too busy to care.

People were constantly coming in or going out and every time the bead-curtains parted Brennan felt a quiver of apprehension. A rear exit? He sweated without even a handkerchief to mop himself, trying to take stock. The obvious move was to make for the British Embassy but he wasn't enamoured of the idea. As a last resort, yes. But now that he had cut himself adrift Lloyd seemed a better bet.

God, how he had chopped and changed towards him. . . . He drew the card from his pocket. Matthew Lloyd, London *Sunday Herald* Hotel Colon: Gloria 46824. On the reverse, written with a ball-point, was: *If not available, try Gloria 73641 and ask for Matt.* . . . At any other time the diminutive might have made

Brennan smile. A vehicle grumbled along the street and he willed it to pass. A juke-box blared a tune he had danced to with Alison the night before and dismay entered him again. In twenty-four hours his world had turned upside down.

Twice, the bartender approached him. He couldn't remain there indefinitely, and money was essential—money for telephoning, money for taxis, money to stave off whatever was shaping. The next time the man came near, Brennan signalled him. Leaning between coloured bottles of *gaseosa*, he said: "Are you interested in a watch?"

Narrow eyes studied him suspiciously. "Why should I be?"

"I wondered."

"What kind of watch?"

"A Rolex." Brennan uncoupled the strap. "I'm not asking much."

In London it had cost him sixty pounds, but he was willing to be robbed. He waited while the man examined it, watching the door, pride gone.

"How many pesos?"

"Fifty." Fifteen pounds, say. He'd never get it.

The man made a noise with his lips like a boiling kettle. He put the watch down and went away; served a succession of beers. Minutes went by. When he returned he said sullenly: "What's wrong with it?"

"Nothing."

"How do I know?"

"It's perfect. The strap's a bit worn, but otherwise—"

"Are you off a ship?"

Brennan nodded, hating every moment of the other's clinical scrutiny.

"American?"

"Yes." A nervous glance towards the entrance as the bead-curtains clattered. "It's a Swiss watch. You won't find a better."

"Fifty pesos?"

"That's right."

The man moved away again, leaving him dangling. He took his time before coming back. "Twenty-five," he said with studied indifference.

It was criminal but Brennan had no option. It wasn't an occasion for haggling. "Very well." He pushed the watch across the counter. "Throw in a beer and it's yours."

He was parched. When the beer came he drank it straight down.

"Is there a telephone here?"

"Next door."

He nodded and left, feeling debased, the bartender's gaze boring into his back. It was a narrow street; its blemishes softened by all shapes and shades of shadow. There was no sign of a hunt, but he felt exposed. PAN-AMERICANO greeted him from the opposite wall and he thought of Merchant with unreasoning viciousness. Merchant was a part of this, too. A tobacconist's adjoined the bar. He entered quickly and bought cigarettes and matches. The telephone was in a corner near the door and he asked the operator to put him through to the Oasis Club. He ached to hear Alison's voice, yet almost dreaded it. What he would say beyond "Why?" he couldn't imagine. But he wanted an answer before he took another step and events closed any further over his head; he at least had the right to that.

"Oasis."

"Room Eight." He was terse, fingers beating a tattoo.

"*Momento*." Dull clicks sounded along the line. Brennan licked his lips, his mind riveted to the humming seconds. They seemed to stretch on and on before he was eventually told: "There is no reply, señor. Do you wish to leave a message?"

He hung up. Resentment swept him again, hardening his heart. There was a rack of postcards near his elbow with flattering views of La Paz at its sun-drenched best and he toyed with the notion of sending her one, writing a question-mark and nothing more—made mean by the sense of abandonment. But caution prevailed.

Gloria 46824 . . . This time he dialled.

"Señor Lloyd?" a girl queried parrot-fashion.

"Please."

Another wait. Distant laughter in the background. Then Lloyd was there. "Yes. Who's calling?"

"It's your German friend."

"Who?—ahhh . . ." He was quick to respond. "How safe's this line?"

"I'm not at the Club, if that's what you mean."

"I see. . . . Well? Something new?"

"I'm in a mess."

A longish pause: a change of tone. "What kind of mess?"

"Pretty bad."

"Because of the car?"

"That was only the beginning."

"Hang on a tick." A booth-door padded softly. Then: "On the back of that card of mine—did I give you an address or a number?"

"A number."

"Well, here's the address. Calle Rafael 42. Got it? Don't write it down. Calle Rafael 42."

"I'd better warn you. Front doors are out."

"Not at Number 42, chum. . . . See you there in about an hour. Save it till then, eh?"

An hour would take some killing, but Brennan didn't demur. He hooked up and lit a cigarette before venturing into the darkness. As he reached for the door-handle he found himself confronted through the glass by an officer of the militia and a momentary panic knotted in the pit of his stomach. Self-control demanded an enormous effort. But then, with a flush of relief, he realised that the officer had stepped back and was smilingly giving him the right of way. Brennan opened the door and pushed past him. "*Gracias*," he muttered. "*Gracias*." He walked a short distance, badly shaken. Patches of light yielded the secret of others who also walked—couples, family groups, a few lone men sauntering without fixed intent, a strutting girl or two. An hour. . . . An hour in which to mark time. And then? He was unable to think beyond the sixty minutes; the immediate pressures. He turned a corner and stood against a wall. He could still change his plans about Lloyd; resort to orthodoxy and present himself at the Embassy. Could, but would not. Cooper's refined incredulity would be more than he could cope with. He was in no mood to trace the tortuous two-day pattern through again—which was what he would have to do: the overall chain of cause and effect was indivisible now. Cooper could wait— and not out of loyalty to Lloyd's desire for secrecy. But with Lloyd at least there was common ground, a devious mind to suggest how to put the night to the best use, a go-between if need be. Tomorrow could look after itself if only Alison would explain.

The thud of running feet caused him to flatten into the shadows. A gang of youths pounded past, shouting meaninglessly. Brennan moved on, unskilled at dawdling, out of place in these narrow streets of the old city. It was a rabbit-warren here, a maze, and the police probably knew better than to waste their energies on it. But even the casual glance of a passer-by seemed filled with meaning. A taxi would take him to the Calle Rafael, wherever it was. Until then he must stay clear of the broad, brightly-lit avenues, avoid needless contacts, keep himself to himself.

An hour—and only a few minutes of it gone. He found another saloon, peering through the windows before entering. The sickly-sweet smell of molasses greeted him. It was a dreary place with a plain tiled floor and brass spittoons beside the tables. His eyes ranged over the people present as he made his way to a seat. They looked safe enough; incurious enough. He sat alone where he could watch the door. There was nothing to be had except rum and beer. Rum he couldn't stomach, so he ordered the other. Whisky or cognac would have suited him better: he was beginning to feel played out. There was an unreal quality about his predicament, a wrong-end-of-the-telescope distortion to what had happened. Sipping his beer, tracing the moisture rings on the table-top, for long seconds on end he seemed almost as if he were reflecting on someone else's dilemma. But when habit made him glance at his left wrist, for instance, and he saw only the pale bare band on the tan where the watch had been there was an end to aberration and his thoughts congealed in ever-fresh amazement around the day's turning-point. "Yes, *guardia*. This is the man" . . . Not even Lloyd's wildest suggestion could ever match the shock of that or more antagonise his will.

There was a telephone near the counter's end. Every time

Brennan looked at it his impatience intensified. He delayed for what he supposed was about a quarter of an hour, then rang the Oasis again. The receptionist was quick to recognise his voice, but the result was the same. No answer. Señora Stacey was not in her room.

"I should like to have her paged, please."

"Very well, señor."

For what seemed like hours he strained to hear the rustle of her coming. At a table next to his four men played cards, colourless rum in their glasses, their mulatto features hard and tense. From the other end of the saloon there was a burst of argument which cut through the general level of conversation. Brennan scarcely noticed either. Where was she? Already dining? In the bar? With Merchant? . . . He roved the building with his mind's eye, willing her to be found. She was unlikely to think it was him. . . . God, was he reduced to that? —sneaking up on her? —catching her unawares?

"I'm sorry, señor, but Señora Stacey does not appear to be in the Club. Is there a message?"

"No."

"Shall I say who called?"

"No."

He returned to the table, nursing frustration, feeling it evolve into a renewal of anger. If she had meant to teach him a lesson she had picked on the wrong man. All at once he wanted Lloyd's hunch to be correct, his armoury stacked with every weapon he could lay hands on. . . . Moodily, Brennan drank, trying to gauge the passing of time, hating the crudeness of his desire to hit back, to score, yet unable to check himself. He finished three beers, brooding, one part of his mind on sentry-go, alert to the ebb and flow of the saloon's trade and any hint of hostile surmise.

In for a penny, in for a pound. . . . Why not? Why the hell not?

His chair screeched as he pushed it back. The clinging aroma of molasses seemed to follow him into the hot night air. He wandered along the street, on the look-out for a taxi. When he was about a hundred yards from the saloon a pulsing neon sign disclosed a trio of soldiers moving his way. Caps askew, arms linked, their off-duty gait a little tipsy, they offered no threat, but Brennan avoided them, turning into the doorway of a *farmacia* until they had gone. At the next intersection he stopped a cruising taxi and got in before giving the driver instructions.

"Calle Rafael."

"Where?"

For a worrying moment Brennan imagined he had heard Lloyd wrongly. "Calle Rafael."

"It's a long one. You can't want the whole of it."

"Forty-two."

The man smirked; flicked down the meter-arm. Brennan had meant to keep the number to himself, but he had lost all sense of direction and had no idea where the street was or what it was like. He lit a cigarette and tried to make sense of the taxi's involved route. He suspected that he was being given the tourist's usual runaround, because nearly a peso was on the clock before he got his bearings. They were running parallel to Conquistador —between blocks he glimpsed a fountain, then a tramcar. A few seconds afterwards, following a wrenching turn that flung him almost across the length of the seat, he realised with sudden astonishment that they were near Vega's, approaching it from the side. Impulsively, he tapped the driver on the shoulder; told him to pull in.

"This isn't the Rafael."

"I know." Brennan opened the door and jumped down. "Wait."

There were more lights hereabouts; a thickening of the Saturday-night crowds. He crossed the road diagonally and hurried to the corner where the blind woman sold lottery tickets, the cautionary whispers dimmed, impelled by a reckless wish to confront Vega while he still had the chance. "Listen, Gabriel," he was going to say. "You didn't fool me this morning. You cooked up those negatives and someone else took the others— isn't that right? That man when I came in was here to see that you did as you were told. That's why you used Spanish, wasn't it? ... Quickly—tell me the truth. Then I'll go." No threats, no scenes. The little monkey-faced man needn't even open his mouth. A nod would suffice. "I'm not blaming you, Gabriel, I didn't know what I think I know now. I've come a long way since this morning. And if you're afraid—well I was never here tonight, understand? You never saw me again after this morning. But, for God's sake, don't hold out on me a second time. . . ."

He turned the corner, careful suddenly. At the most he expected a loitering policeman, but for as far as he could see the sidewalk was clear of danger. Then, to his astonishment, he realised that the shop was closed, the windows shuttered, the door-blind down. Not a slit of light showed anywhere. He tried the door, but it was locked. He had been so confident of entry that he stepped back, puzzled, and stared up at the emblazoned sign, half-suspecting that he must have come to the wrong place. But there it was—VEGA—scripted in blue neon over the shop-front. Shut?—at this hour? . . . He couldn't afford to linger. He turned away, cheated, disturbed.

"Luck," the blind woman called. "Buy yourself luck."

Brennan paused, unmoved by the despair in the cry. "How long has Vega's been closed?"

She gazed through him with eyes like opals. "Since noon, señor."

"Are you sure?"

"Since noon. Soon after you left."

"*I?*"

"I recognise your voice. Last night you were kind to me."

Brennan hesitated, thinking unworthy things, beyond the reach of charity. "That was last night. We didn't speak this morning."

"I also know your step. You have been here several times." Her nostrils flared as if she were smelling him, as if to show that she wasn't as imprisoned as he believed.

"At noon, you say?"

"Two men came in a car. After the shutters were pulled up the señor went away with them."

"Señor Vega?"

"Yes."

"Who were these men?"

113

She spread her dark hands and the soiled tickets fluttered, pink and green. "How should I know, señor? The world is full of strangers. But I have lived with Señor Vega's walk for many years and I could not be wrong about him." A cough racked her. "There is sickness in his family, perhaps."

Brennan's coin rattled in the metal cup. He left her abruptly, deaf to the pursuing litany of thanks, sensing the underlying drama as never before. Something close to fear brushed lightly over his nerves. The taxi was waiting for him by the opposite kerb and he ran to it, grateful for its sanctuary and the prospect of rejoining Lloyd. For too long he had thought in terms of a private quarrel; catch-as-catch-can, ominous but unskilled. But at last he was convinced. A kind of war was on, and there were casualties to prove it.

CHAPTER TEN

THE Calle Rafael was every bit as long as the driver had intimated. To begin with there was a concentration of bowling alleys, cinemas and dance-halls; then came a seemingly unending succession of apartment houses, many with ROOM TO LET signs, followed by block after block of terraced façades, their multi-coloured tints paled by the harsh, sodium-white glare of street-lamps. Brennan sat forward on the cracked leather seat, peering to either side. He couldn't read the numbers of the houses. Groups of people were sometimes congregated on the steps, gossiping, lolling, soaked with heat—shirtless men, women with their hair in curlers. Barefooted children scampered from one flight, one garbage bin, to another. The traffic had diminished along with the crowds. It was quiet here; quiet enough for heads to turn as the taxi passed. Brennan sweated, alerted by the day's final assault on his senses. It was a bad time to know nothing of his destination except an address and the longer the journey lasted the more anxious he became. Two more blocks went by with a gaunt church sandwiched in between. Then, at last, the taxi nosed into the gutter and juddered to a halt in front of a pink-washed house named Casa Abril.

"Is this it?" It would be madness to be stranded in the wrong place. "Number Forty-two?"

"It's one and the same."

Brennan parted with two pesos fifty, staring at the house again as he did so. Only then did he get out.

"I assure you," the man said, misinterpreting Brennan's nervousness. "Not the moment for a mistake, eh?" he added cryptically, all teeth and crinkled eyes, then pulled away with a derisive double-bleat of the horn.

A yellowish cat fled from the steps as Brennan mounted them. It was a three-storeyed house with numerous grilled windows. The door was of frosted glass built into a heavy wrought-iron frame. The bell consisted of a pulley contraption fixed above the glazed name-plaque on the wall. Light blurred softly through the glass and Brennan thought he could hear music. A spasm of distrust took hold of him and for a second or two he delayed. A marked effort seemed required to reach up and grasp the pulley. Only then did he notice that "42" was embossed on the lintel. He yanked the pulley twice, then waited, watching the street uneasily. A Vespa phut-phutted where the block ended: close at hand the cat mewed. With a throb of expectancy he saw a shadow fall on the glass from within; shrink and focus into an approximation of human shape. A catch clicked. Then the door was opened a foot or two and a large, olive-skinned woman in a bright green dress confronted him. She was middle-aged, fleshy, with a drinker's face. Not all of her showed in the space she had allowed herself.

"*Si?*" she said. Her sloe-black eyes were wary.

"I was told to ask for Matt."

"Matt? . . . Ah, *si*." She motioned him in.

Brennan found himself enclosed by a neat, square lobby. A fan revolved overhead. Tiled floor, rubber plants in brass bowls, framed splashes of colour on pastel walls—a degree of relief sharpened his awareness. The woman shut the door and dropped the catch. She smiled as she turned, her eyes pouching. Her hair was short and silvery-pink; her perfume over-strong.

"You're a friend of Matt's?" Now she spoke English, her accent thick, the rhythm slovenly.

"That's right."

"Matt's a nice guy. He calls quite a lot."

"I'd like to see him."

She smiled again, weighing him up. It was dawning on him what she was; where he had come. He followed her past a curving staircase into a softly-lit room of surprising elegance, cool and spacious. Music came from a cabinet record-player. There was a quilted bar in one corner: windows, flung wide, opened on to what looked like a flagged patio. Somewhere in the house a girl laughed.

"Is Matt here?" The more Brennan used the diminutive the more unreal it seemed.

"You thought he would be?"

"Yes."

The woman shrugged and pouted simultaneously. "What are we going to know you as?"

"I'm sorry?"

"What do we call you, honey?"

"Harry."

Her gaze was a continuing assessment of him. "Harry," she said. "That's very nice. And Matt's a friend of yours, yes?"

He nodded. She would have been beautiful once.

"Can I fix you a drink?"

"Not at the moment." He glanced round, nerves far from slackened off. Lloyd certainly picked his places. An explanation seemed necessary, and he said: "I'm afraid I'm here under false pretences."

"You needn't be."

"It was Matt I came to see."

"That's up to you, Harry."

"He asked me to meet him here."

"Are you another journalist?"

"No."

"Matt's a lively specimen, I must say." She chuckled, as if prompted by a memory. "We've had some arguments, he and I. He likes a good argument. It's sometimes all he comes for.

Ayee, he's an interesting one. Generous, too." She moved to the bar. "You'll wait for him, I suppose?"

"If I may."

"Sure. Perhaps you'll change your mind about that drink?"

"Perhaps I will."

"A *daiquiri*?"

"Scotch, if it's possible."

"Everything is possible in the Casa Abril, Harry." She was at ease with strangers; friendly, direct—and as hard as nails. "And if you change your mind about the girls you've only to say. If Matt doesn't show up, for instance. It's ten pesos for the short time. Anything else by arrangement."

"He'll be here."

The bell chimed as he spoke. There was a house-phone on the bar and the woman lifted it. "Take the door, Carmen." Then, her eyes pouching at Brennan, she reverted to English. "How is it you say?—'Mention the Devil. . .?' "

But it wasn't Lloyd. A raven-haired girl in lilac rustled past the end of the room and made for the lobby. There were sounds of the door opening and closing; a muttered conversation. "Pardon me a moment," the woman said and left Brennan to his whisky. He drank, unrelaxed, thinking of the time and what could have delayed Lloyd. Finding himself here was no more improbable than anything else that had happened. The breathing-space was welcome, but he couldn't blink the facts. He was on the run; in need of help. He glimpsed a portly man going up the stairs with the girl in lilac, his problem solved; heard laughter again, and—in a break in the music as a record changed —the rasp of cicadas from beyond the patio windows. Dully, as the woman returned, he realised that he could not remember what desire was. Alison seemed to have frozen his by acting as she had, and by remaining inaccessible. Yet for her to enter his mind was like having a bruise pummelled, pain and memory intermingling. Even his ability to speculate had foundered now.

"Tell me," he said. "How late is it?"

"Ten to nine." The woman chuckled again, deep-throated, like a boy whose voice is breaking. "You're really on a rack, aren't you? Does Matt owe you money or something?"

Brennan lifted his shoulders like a piano-player.

"Don't worry, honey. There's no rush." She retrieved her *daiquiri*. "How long have you been in Santa Marta?"

"Long enough."

"Don't you like it? Or doesn't it like you?"

"That's a big question."

She was on the verge of prying and he fenced with her, careful when he lied to lie sensibly. By nine o'clock he had about reached the end of his chain. Five minutes more and he would probably have telephoned Lloyd's hotel; that, or taken it into his head to risk the streets again and make for the Embassy. But the bell sounded just as he was beginning to think it never would, and Lloyd arrived—a strangely boisterous Lloyd, holding the woman's arm, old friend, old client, able to tease and joke, calling her "*señora mia*".

She said: "Harry's been sweating for you like you were never going to be here. Haven't you, Harry?"

"You won't believe it, but the car played up on me. Still—better late than never, I hope." Playfully, Lloyd smacked the woman's rump. "How about the welcoming glass, *señora mia*?"

"Of course, of course."

"She's a treasure," Lloyd grinned. "Aren't you, darling? Beyond price."

"If you say so." With a twinkling glance at Brennan, she said: "Matt's always full of fun. Some are so sad and solemn that I sometimes think they've come to the wrong place. But not Matt." Across the bar she pinched his cheek.

"I know where I'm appreciated, that's why." He was drinking beer. "Long live the Casa Abril—and all who fail in her."

Impatiently, Brennan waited for Lloyd to finish brandishing his libido. He was desperately anixous to unburden himself, but Lloyd was in no great hurry to let him. How much his manner was calculated was impossible to say, but he was a different man from the one who'd gone to Pozoblanco with him—prurient, gay, apparently indifferent to Brennan's plight, content to prolong the banter. If he sensed Brennan's restlessness he gave no indication of it. Every remark, every guffaw, implied that this was the life. It seemed a long time before he eventually said:

"*Señora mia*, where's somewhere I can have a talk with my friend?"

"There's always a room."

"Okay."

"How long will you be?"

"We'll see, shall we? I'll get around to calling you an extortionate so-and-and-so afterwards—how's that?"

"Since it's you, Matt."

"No wonder I love you, darling."

"Come," the woman said.

They followed her thick ankles up to the first floor. It was a small room, narrow, with a double bed, a brocaded dressing-table and two full-length mirrors. She switched on the fan and dropped the slatted blinds. Her parting smile flickered quizzically over them both. "Satisfactory, yes?"

Lloyd waited several seconds after the door was shut before speaking. Quietly, with an explanatory shrug, he said: "She needs humouring, you know. A little blarney and you're home and dried."

"You do it damn well."

His mouth slipped sideways. "Does it show so much?" Now there was weakness visible in him again, self-doubt, the accumulated stresses since the days of the Imjin River. "No excuses. It gives me a kick to keep coming. Everything else gets harder, but a place like this—"

"I wasn't being smug."

"It's worth dredging from time to time, in any case. Remember that rumour I told you about?"

"The plane?"

Lloyd nodded. "This is where I raked it up. Generally speaking a solid find's as scarce as a fly at the North Pole. But for once my stars were bright and shining." He offered Brennan a cigarette; the smoke swirled. Through it he said: "I never thought you'd ring. My feeling was that you'd gone sour on me."

"I had."

"Why did you change your mind?"

"It was changed for me."

"What exactly happened? A to Z, please."

Lloyd subsided on to the bed. Once he grunted; once he whistled. But he didn't interrupt. Brennan kept his voice low. If he had been able to analyse his tone he would have noticed how, when he referred to Alison, it was with continuing amazement; whereas Vega's arrest he recounted in a level, matter-of-fact fashion that was indicative of the way his mind had swung. For the first time he was a stepping-stone ahead of Lloyd, the shock of Vega already absorbed. Lloyd's surprised grunt came early, when Brennan described the scene with Alison at the Oasis: but his drawn-out whistle was reserved for the end.

"Vega, eh?" He heaved himself into a sitting position. "My God, I might have guessed. And I was going there later. If you hadn't rung me I'd have been along there tonight, on the off-chance of dazzling him with some *Herald* expense-money. My God," he repeated, "they certainly didn't waste any time. Poor Mr. Bloody Vega." His eyes glinted. "Now who's chasing a will-o'-the-wisp?"

"You win," Brennan said. "I've come off the fence."

"And fallen into a decidedly sticky mess."

"You can say that again."

"Don't worry. We'll work something out."

"It's beyond me."

"About López and his foreign friends? Nothing else fits the facts. It may not have been a very clever ploy to invite them in but it was probably the smartest bird-in-the-hand bit of blackmail he could think up at the time."

Brennan shook his head. "I'm talking about the car." He moved restlessly.

"Ah, yes, sorry. I can see we've got different priorities." Lloyd stood up and began to pace. "Did she know where you'd been? Why you'd taken it?"

"I don't believe so. She'd pooh-poohed my suspicions, anyway —about my room having been searched and the film deliberately tampered with and my being followed. She and Merchant laughed them off from the start."

"Merchant . . . American Embassy man? Is that his name?"

"Yes."

"I didn't know you'd discussed anything with either of them."

"Hell, I'm not a Trappist. And when I came back from Vega's"—was it only that morning?—"I was pretty mad. Merchant's attitude didn't exactly help, either. He triggers me off at the best of times as it is. But I don't think *she* was angry until that fellow went into the pool. Even so, just because I borrowed her car . . ." Defeated, Brennan ran a hand through his hair, back where he always finished.

Lloyd said: "I'm no Mr. Lonely-Hearts, chum. But as you may have noticed I'm a great guesser."

"Go on."

"D'you mind if I ask you a personal question? It presupposes that you're in love with the young lady, so perhaps you'll tell me to stuff my mouth."

"What is it?"

"Is she in love with you?"

"I thought so. I was hoping so."

"Then isn't it possible that she did what she did because she was thinking of your safety?"

Already, during his hour at large in the back streets, this thought had occurred to Brennan; formed the basis of a vague and slender hope. But it hadn't seemed to bear examination. Lloyd was too damned slick with his formulas. Love was an exchange between equals, neither tit for tat nor something at the mercy of half-formulated fears. . . . He felt very tired now, reaction setting in. Wearily, he said: "You're presupposing something else."

"What?"

"That she believed everything I told her. And even if she did—which I doubt—then why in the blazes should she decide to throw me to the wolves? She must have realised it would suit them. 'Something innocuous to nail you with'—they're your words."

"She could have withdrawn the charge tomorrow, say, and you'd hardly have had a scar to show for it." Lloyd stubbed his cigarette in a tray. "How was she to know that you were going to take to your heels and turn yourself into an Aunt Sally for López's merry men? A night or two in the cooler is better than a bullet in the back. That's the risk you're running from now on—and what I suspect the young lady wanted to save you from. She probably knows you're an obstinate cuss."

Voices sounded from another room. Someone was happy.

"Listen, chum. You've had the luck of Old Nick this evening, getting clear the way you did, but if the heat's on now you're the one who turned the tap. Put yourself in their position. And remember that what they lack in efficiency they make up for with persistence and ruthlessness. People disappear without trace in Santa Marta as easily as a pint of porter goes down in Dublin City."

Brennan stood by the window, plucking the blind. "I want to get in touch with her."

"Don't try."

"I've tried already."

"By phone?"

"Twice."

Lloyd snorted. "You're a lunatic."

"It was before I knew about Vega."

"Even so, you're a lunatic. They'll be sitting on her tail as much as they were on yours."

"After what she's done?"

"They can't afford to give anyone the benefit of the doubt. Besides, she's a sort of bait for you. They may be clumsy, but their basic psychology's sound."

"You're so sure, aren't you? Always so sure." Brennan glared across the bed. "I've got to contact her. That's more important to me right now than anything else."

"If you attempt it from here they'll trace the call and be down on you quicker than the Assyrian jumped the fold. On her, too, probably. Make a run for the British Embassy and they'll pick you up fifty yards from the steps. They can pull you out of there, anyhow, since you unfortunately don't belong: there's blank space on the map in the foyer to prove it." Lloyd lit another cigarette. "If you're wise you'll stay where you are and keep away from the telephone as if it were the plague."

"Here?"

"Why not? People do, you know."

"For how long?"

"Long enough for me to be your errand-boy and see what I can—"

Something thudded against the window-grille. It could only have been a bat, but they both started. Lloyd moistened his lips and the cigarette trembled slightly in his fingers as he went on. "Except for a Press attaché who hates my guts on principle and a natural Palace suspicion of the *Herald*'s tendency to reveal the sordid my nose is currently clean. They won't have a clue who was with you at Pozoblanco. To coin a phrase, I continue to enjoy unrestricted freedom of movement. But where else is there for you?"

He was most nearly himself when his nerves were jolted. Downstairs, with the woman, he had come close to caricature. But now, with endeavoured coolness, clinging to some remnant of former confidence, he unintentionally achieved greater honesty. Tired and confused though Brennan was he noticed the flaw in him once again. Yet, for all that, Lloyd had lost none of his power to persuade. Already the future was pressing in, demanding attention. Tomorrow and what came after couldn't be shelved.

"You'd be cutting off your nose to spite your face, chum; I kid you not."

"Would you see that she gets a letter?"

"It may not be easy."

"All you'd have to do—"

"I'm in a priviliged position. I don't want it compromised." Lloyd offered a mitigating gesture. "Don't misunderstand me. I'll help all I can, but slipping messages under doors or leaving them with desk-clerks is asking for interception. The only way to deliver a letter is person to person, and I wouldn't chance it if she's being watched."

"You'll try, though?"

"Sure, I'll try. But I don't guarantee delivery." He gave Brennan his pen and some paper torn from a notebook. "I'll say this. If I were in your shoes I'd be wondering about one thing and one thing only—how I was going to get clear of Santa Marta." He paused. "That's what it comes to—don't you realise?"

Three times Brennan tried to put something down. He

couldn't even begin to set his mind in order. Anger had gone and dismay had staled. It was no better than asking questions of himself; like scrawling explanations on the walls of a cell. *I can only think there has been a ghastly misunderstanding . . . It was stupid and unthinking of me to take your car, I realise, but the Land-Rover . . .* One minute with her and he would know where he stood, but—written—the self-same phrases were inadequate as they were impersonal. *God knows what happens next. I'm holed up for the time being, and the way things are shaping . . .* It was no use. For the third time he screwed the paper into a ball, unable to decide which Alison he was trying to reach. It was unreal to think of her as being so close, a mile away at most, and yet so unattainable.

Lloyd watched him from the bed. "No good?"

He shook his head; glanced through the blinds, weighing the temptation of the dark streets.

"Don't try it," Lloyd said with more bite than before. "Listen. I'm about twenty-four hours short of what I want. Somewhere in this city are three bodies—two broken up, one intact. If one of the Casa Abril's dark-haired darlings were to produce a packet of Russian cigarettes left by a pilfering member of that helicopter team I'd maybe say: Okay, I won't press my luck any more. This is proof enough . . . But it won't happen. I've got to rout around for myself. There are three bodies lying about somewhere and it's up to me to find out where and who they are."

"Then what?"

"Then you and I skedaddle."

Brennan almost jeered. "Just like that?"

"It can be arranged, Practically anything in Santa Marta can be arranged, from an election to a murder. *Vide* López. A nice little sea trip will put colour back in both our cheeks." Lloyd smiled loosely, as if masking an incipient dread. "You're as safe here as you could be anywhere. Meanwhile, yours truly has got work to do."

"What about Alison? I'm not staying cooped up—"

"You haven't tried blowing your brains out, either. Look; if I can get word to her, I will. But time's on the go and the dead don't keep in this climate. If she put the handcuffs on you for the reason I think she did, then you ought to be flattered. Amongst other things it means that she took in what you told her. What's more, it means that Mr. Merchant from the American Embassy took it in, too. You aren't the only one with a crisis on hand Old Lloyd's Almanac reckons there's a top-level game of cat-and-mouse already well under way." He rose, preparing to leave. "I'll be back in the morning. Get some sleep. You're beginning to look as if you need it. And, no matter what, let me find you here when I come."

Grudgingly, Brennan nodded.

"I'm not asking it just for your sake, chum, believe me. If you're hungry or want a drink something can be sent up. Make yourself at home, in fact. I'll fix the overheads, don't worry." At the door, he paused. "Incidentally—can you recommend a small camera that won't break the bank?"

"What sort of bank?"

"The seventy-five, hundred-peso mark."

"They're all pretty useful." It was only after Brennan had made a few automatic suggestions, after he had followed Lloyd on to the landing and was watching him descend the staircase, that he called out "What d'you want it for?" To which Lloyd merely put a finger against his lips and continued on down.

The door-bell rang from time to time, discreet voices sounded, footsteps came close and went away. Brennan had no wish to eat. After what might have been half an hour he went in search of somewhere to wash, then returned to the room and locked himself in. For a long time sleep was out of the question. Without coat or shoes he lay on the bed with the lights out and stared through the slats at the sky-glow of La Paz. In spite of everything it was difficult to feel menaced, but a mood of blackest melancholy possessed him, complex and unyielding. Lloyd was for ever ready with a plausible explanation, but what he had suggested on Alison's behalf Brennan would only believe when he heard it from her own lips. And how this would be possible if tomorrow or the day after meant being somehow smuggled off the island he couldn't imagine.

When at last he slept it was badly, never far from the surface.

Night long he seemed to be waking, thoughts swarming consciously around Alison; though once there was a hillside of humming-birds—and Vega, who was with him, shouting in alarm: "Watch out, Mr. Brennan! Watch out!"

CHAPTER ELEVEN

THE morning sky was ribbed with cloud. Within seconds of rousing Brennan was at the window, discovering where the house was in relation to the Cathedral of the Sacred Heart and the Presidential Palace; deducing the Oasis Club's direction and the rough location of the British Embassy. There wasn't much of a view, but orientation added a realistic dimension to the day's beginning. He had no idea of the hour, but a bell was ringing—not in the house; a church bell—and along the Calle Rafael he glimpsed some children going in white to their first Communion like doll brides and toy soldiers. He had almost forgotten what peace of mind was.

The Casa Abril was deep in an exhausted quiet. The silence contained no threat, but as time passed he was torn with all the old uncertainties. The screwed-up notes he had tried to write Alison lay on the dressing-table like symbols of defeat and Lloyd's cigarette-ends filled the only ashtray. He had wearied of speculation; worn his mind threadbare. There were exasperated moments when it struck him as preposterous that he should continue to remain imprisoned and wait passively for Lloyd to return: but mostly he accepted the necessity, Vega's arrest a warning, the alternatives vague. It was disturbing to be grateful yet to know that his own dilemma was incidental to the issues which concerned Lloyd. Disturbing, too, to have only a lukewarm confidence in Lloyd's capabilities. Beggars couldn't be choosers—and last evening he had as good as thrown himself on his mercy. But there was no telling where it would lead, and Lloyd's obvious forcing of himself—the jaunty manner, the slightly dated verbal bravado, with which he camouflaged a potential failure of nerve—wasn't encouraging.

Hunger eventually drove Brennan out on to the landing. He looked over the balustrade, but saw no signs of life. Presently, on his way to the bathroom, he cannoned into a sleep-sodden girl padding barefoot along the corridor. "*Hola*," she murmured thickly, unmindful of her gaping robe. He returned the greeting, hesitated, then asked what time it was and how he could get something to eat. The time she didn't know, and the thought of food evidently repelled her because she screwed her smudged face and moved away. Later, though, when Brennan was back in his room, there was a knock and a voice said: "Nine thirty . . . And it's Sunday"—as if oblivion inevitably followed bought solace. Later still there was another knock, which took him to the door. The woman with the silver-pink hair and pouchy eyes greeted him.

"Matt rang and asked to tell you he won't be long." She was sluttish in the light of day; older looking, harder, badly in need of the morning's convalescence. "D'you want some coffee?"

"Please."

"I'll have it brought up." She frowned. "Will you be leaving soon?"

"I can't say. It depends."

"What's keeping you?" The tone was none too warm. "I run a house, Harry. So long as a man pays—and behaves—okay: I don't pry. But if there's trouble, or could be trouble—" She spread her podgy hands. "Understand?"

"There won't be."

"Is it business of some kind?"

"That's right," he said guardedly. "You ask Matt if it worries you."

Off his own tongue the name still had the unnaturalness of a password. The woman gave him a lengthy, doubting look before going. He crossed to his point of vigil at the window and lit one of two remaining cigarettes, anxious, stroking his bristle, watching the Calle Rafael, wondering about Lloyd and what he had been able to achieve; what he might propose when he came. The illusion of security was already undermined. Nowhere was safe—a place without loyalties least of all. A whim, a suspicion, a dislike—and no matter how good your money you could be out in the street.

An elderly coloured maid brought him a tray not long afterwards and set it impassively on the dressing-table; departed without a word or a glance. There was coffee with claw-shaped rolls and whitish butter. He ate ravenously, then lay on the bed, trying to keep a hold on his patience. When a police-wagon sirened along the street he got up quickly; felt a surge of relief when he saw it disappear. The sun burned between drifting bars of cloud and the shadows ebbed and flowed. A flag moved sluggishly above the distant Palace; laundry on scores of flat, tenement roof-tops. Over the heart of the city the speck of a kite was riding the up-currents, wheeling, biding its time. Ten o'clock yet? Ten thirty? . . . No day had ever been so reluctant to move.

It must have been near to eleven before he heard the street-bell, followed by the sound of Lloyd's voice. He went out on to the landing at once, never more glad to see anyone. Lloyd was in his bouncing, thigh-pinching mood, but the woman had cooled noticeably. "*Buenos dias, amigo,*" Lloyd called, catching sight of him. "How's my darling attended to your welfare?"

"Matt," he heard the woman say, "I want to talk with you."

"Of course. Nothing I'd like better. But afterwards, eh? After I've listed my friend's complaints. How about that?"

She shrugged, tight-lipped, unamused.

Lloyd patted her on the arm and started up the stairs, turning theatrically half-way to blow her a kiss. "You're a marvel, *señora mia*, and I love you dearly."

He winked at Brennan as he reached the landing, preceded him into the bedroom. He was wheezing slightly and leaned against the closed door.

"She wants me out of here," Brennan said.

"She's just got a Sunday morning hangover."

"Maybe. But she wants me out all the same."

"I'll nudge her round in a bit."

"I wouldn't be too sure."

"She'll play until this evening, or—forgive me—I've lost my charm."

"And then?"

"With any luck, action stations." Lloyd sat on the bed and mopped his face. "You'll be pleased to hear I've been busy. By this time tomorrow you and I stand a fair chance of being in Kingston, Jamaica."

The future could wait for the moment. "Did you contact Alison?"

"No. And I'll be honest; I didn't even try. But I did what was probably the soundest thing—I had a word with that fellow Merchant."

"Oh?"

"A very smooth young man indeed. Right on the ball and giving absolutely nothing away. Yes, he knew you: why, yes, you were the gentleman who'd been in some kind of trouble over Miss Stacey's car." Lloyd smiled, fingering the broad, frayed line of his parting. "He didn't as much as bat an eye when I told him that you'd objected to being arrested and had cut loose. But it knocked him. The ash dropped off his cigarette as if a shock wave had gone along his arm."

"Where was this?"

"At the Oasis last night. He tried to pump me, which was difficult in the circumstances because he was also trying to indicate that he couldn't really care less. However, I wasn't having any. I merely said that you were most anxious to get in touch with the lady in question and would he please do his damnedest to make it possible."

"And—"

"I offered myself as a *poste restante* and gradually implied that I hadn't a clue what it was all about, either. I'm meeting him again at noon."

Brennan sucked in air. "Thanks."

"It's the best I could do, chum." Lloyd squinted through the window. The view seemed to shrink as a cloud dragged over the sun. "I also approached a certain Johnny about running us across the water. It's not as cloak-and-dagger as you might think. There's a thriving invisible import-export business in these parts. He's thinking it over."

"Why 'us'?" Brennan said. "I don't see why you have to sneak through the back door."

"I might have to when the time comes. Anyhow, I'm all for company. And, in any case, it'll add a touch of flavour—Lloyd was there to the last, and all that crap." He offered Brennan a cigarette. "By the way—about that camera: I got a 35-mm. Yashica. Any good?"

"For the money."

"Flash attachment and all—eighty-six pesos. I'll show it you later. I suppose you've guessed why I want it?"

Brennan nodded. "And I think you're either out of your mind or rank as the biggest optimist I've ever struck. You don't even know where the bodies are."

"I've a shrewd if unoriginal idea."

"Where?"

"Where they'd normally be—at the morgue. I've just cruised round a couple of times, ostensibly to have a look at the fire damage to La Granja market, and there's an army guard on the building."

"Perhaps there is always."

"No." Lloyd was adamant. "It's tucked away inside the main doors—though the need for fresh air seemed to have defeated any intention to be discreet."

"Then you're even crazier than I thought."

"You could be right at that." The church along the Calle Rafael was clanging its great green bell again, and with a grin shaped by nerves Lloyd said: "After this I'm going to ask for a seat behind a desk and buy myself a season-ticket on the 8.55. But whether I like it or not, chum, for me this is a day of obligation."

He left ten minutes or so afterwards, promising to return at about three. From the bedroom door Brennan heard him cajoling the woman with bawdy archness, lowering his voice as he took her into his confidence on some trumped-up story of an exclusive; of wanting to keep Brennan clear of 'the pack'. Presently he came up the stairs, on the pretence of having left his cigarettes behind but in reality to whisper: "You're right.

She's on edge about you—don't ask me why. Maybe you've hurt her professional pride by not sampling her wares. But if she gets difficult before I turn up, push off. Go to the Terana Cinema at the end of the street and wait for me there, back of the circle." Then he was gone again, with unhealthy eagerness. The front of the house wasn't visible from the window, but after a few moments Brennan saw the familiar black saloon sweeping up the Calle Rafael in the direction of Conquistador.

Left to himself Brennan reflected ruefully on the way in which chance was aligning his allies. It was impossible to think of Frank Merchant without gall; and the more Lloyd revealed his intentions so Brennan found himself selfishly regretting that he wasn't dependent on someone less obsessed. Merchant was the last person he had ever imagined would do him a useful service, but the irony that it should be in connection with Alison wasn't as disturbing as the prospect of Lloyd's declared grand-slam. Vega's abduction had opened his eyes. Now when Alison entered his mind it was in company with Merchant—and Merchant led on to Lloyd, Lloyd to Vega, Vega to the unknown in the ceiba tree. Whichever way his thoughts turned, from whichever point they started, the permutation was inescapable. Lloyd—Vega—Alison—Merchant: Vega—Merchant—Alison Lloyd. . . . And each post-mortem brought him back to the grotesque fluke that had set everything in train.

When he gazed out on the city's Sunday-morning peace it didn't deceive him. Danger was lying in wait as surely as the flag fluttered over the Palace, and he was ready to believe that events were shaping of which he was scarcely a continuing part. It had to be so if Santa Marta were at the mercy of history. He and Lloyd weren't the only ones to be aware of what had happened in Los Colmillos. Vega—Merchant . . . Pan-Americano Merchant. Ears-close-to-the-ground Merchant. Tennis-court Merchant . . . His tired mind circled on. All right; Merchant knew. The American Embassy knew. Washington knew. At a pinch he could make out a case for Merchant's behaviour. But Alison's smarted like an open wound. Good God, he wasn't a child. . . . Brooding got him nowhere though. He could hope, but he couldn't understand. The past was too close on his heels. As for the future he was in Lloyd's hands, and that alone was beginning to be worry enough.

The street-bell began to sound intermittently from what Brennan imagined was about noon onwards. Once he heard English spoken and, going cautiously to his door, he saw a burly U.S. Marine sergeant heading up the stairs with a ferocious-looking blonde. How easy and uncomplicated some escapes could be. He lay on the bed for a while, wishing the time away, hungry again, wondering how long the woman would give him. Presently, as if his anxiety had been transmitted, there was a knock and she was waiting when he turned the key, the night's facial ravages smoothed over.

"About the room—" she began, fresh lips redder than blood.

"Yes?"

"When's Matt due back?"

"At three."

"I want it before then." She was sullen now; sullen and dangerous.

"How soon?"

"At once. Someone's in need of it."

She was lying, but he was in no position to argue. And money wouldn't interest her: whatever instinct prompted her was deep and inflexible, beyond the reach of cash. Lloyd might have tried to small-talk her round and gain an hour or so, but Brennan was split with distrust. Her ultimate remedy was the police, and even if she relented to his face he knew that every time the street-bell rang it would suggest that he had been betrayed.

He shrugged, conscious of his crumpled suit and lack of a shave. "If that's the way you want it."

Her eyes were quite merciless. "No hard feelings."

"Okay." Pride was a luxury he could no longer afford. He shrugged again.

"Where shall I tell Matt to find you?"

"He'll know."

She softened a trifle after they had gone down the stairs. "I'm glad you understand, Harry. You're a nice guy, sure you are, but I don't want trouble."

With a spark of defiance as she showed him out he retorted: "Who said anything about trouble?" Then the door was shut and the burning street was his, the sudden fugitive feeling stronger by daylight than ever before.

He turned in the direction the taxi had brought him the previous night, walking briskly, unmindful of the heat. The Calle Rafael seemed to narrow endlessly into the distance. It was impossible not to believe that every passer-by, far from being caught up in the hard self-sufficiency of life, was a potential informer. He looked ahead for uniforms or a cruising police-wagon, nerves strung taut. It was all of half a mile to the Terana Cinema, but it seemed enormously longer: he thought the blocks of terraced rooming-houses would never end. No taxi came to his rescue now. Where the dingy shops began a man left the wall against which he had been leaning and approached him, asking for a light. In the awful moment before the man spoke Brennan's heart missed a beat and dread clenched in his chest: afterwards his pulse throbbed so violently that it all but drowned the sound of traffic. The crowds thickened a little once he reached the shops and pavement cafés. Mostly, the shops were shut, but the cafés were busy. A clock showed ten minutes after one. Brennan walked on, sweating now, averting his head as he passed the groups of café tables, conscious of the slightest show of interest in him: even to be singled out by a toothless beggar who pleaded from crutches in the gutter seemed like a public accusation. He passed the first of the dance-halls, then a bowling-alley. There were loiterers here, touts, riff-raff, sweetmeat stalls under the jutting canopies, street-photographers, a swirl of people, noise and smells. SI LÓPEZ SI.

The Terana Cinema was barely a block away, but he wasn't safe yet. It had a narrow entrance, garishly bright and as cool as the inside of a well. Brennan bought a circle ticket and walked up; pushed through some curtains and, half-blind, groped in the wake of a swinging torch to the first seat he could find. Cary Grant was on the screen, muttering improbably in dubbed Spanish. Brennan leaned back while his eyes adjusted themselves. Soon he could make out enough to look round. There were scarcely a dozen people in the whole circle, dotted about as

133

if each of them feared contamination from the other, and after a little while he got up and moved to the very back under the fraying fingers of light flooding out from the projection-slots.

No picture had ever seemed more unreal. To Brennan it was like watching a dream from within the framework of another. He sat and waited for Lloyd, alerted whenever anyone came in. There was a clock away to the right of the screen and there were times when he felt sure that it must have stopped. Whatever tensions and suspense the picture offered were smothered by his own. Expectantly he studied the silhouette of every newcomer, vainly willing it to be Lloyd's. It was strange to be so eager to renew contact with someone whose flaws were so transparent and ambitions so rash. A young couple occupied the seats to one side of him and he moved again, this time to the end of the row, peanut husks crunching underfoot. The Cary Grant picture ended and the house-lights swelled through a ceiling of false stars; dim though they were he felt as if they were focused on to him. Presently they faded and the second feature came on. Only two forty. He bought cigarettes from an attendant and smoked, fingers restless, mind restless, vaguely aware of an Hawaiian travelogue but with thoughts for ever following the same frustrating orbit of doubt and uncertainty. He couldn't believe that Lloyd would fail him, but anxiety demanded punctuality and 'about three' had set a limit on what was left of his patience. When the hour came and went an almost intolerable strain possessed him. Twice he persuaded someone that the seat beside him was reserved. Later he had to stand to allow an air force lieutenant and his family to squeeze past along the row. The lieutenant grunted his thanks, and Brennan felt the unreality of his predicament more keenly than ever.

Hawaii vanished in a blazing, crab-red sunset and to the sob of electric guitars. Three fifteen . . . The programme had gone full circle. The Cary Grant credits were filling the screen when Brennan realised that at last it really was Lloyd who was mounting the gangway. Relief made him incautious. He signalled with a wave of his lighted cigarette and Lloyd blundered in alongside, wheezing an almost inaudible: "Like a stack of black cats in here." They sat for several minutes in silence before he spoke again. Then, lips to Brennan's ear, he said: "I gather she turfed you out."

"She did indeed."

"Old bitch. Not to worry. No harm done." He touched Brennan on the knee. "For you."

Brennan found himself clutching an envelope. Peering close he could just make out his own name, but the writing he did not recognise.

"Take it to the gents," Lloyd murmured. "You'll never tell A from a bull's foot in this benighted place."

A woman in front turned with a hiss and a furious gesture. Lloyd spread his hands in apology. "Go on," he mouthed, nudging Brennan and Brennan rose; made his way towards the door marked CABALLEROS. He had the place to himself and entered one of the cubicles. There, leaning against the rough stone wall with its scrawled obscenities, he stared again at the envelope, then slit it open with his thumb and extracted the letter.

> *Dearest Harry:*
>
> *Will you ever forgive me? I've so much to explain if only you will let me, but now isn't the time. Frank's going to sort out the mess. Do as he says, exactly as he says, and everything will be all right. I blame myself for what's happened, so don't act out of anger towards me. I hated what I did, but I truly thought it was for the best. You must believe that.*
>
> *Alison*

He read the note a couple of times before shoving it into a pocket. *Dearest Harry* . . . For a night and a morning and part of an afternoon he had asked for contact—her voice, her presence. . . . An indeterminate emotion swept him, more a purging of resentment than any positive springing-up of joy or relief. It was excusable to have misjudged her; excusable to have given way to all the retaliatory moods that shock and humiliation offered. Not once had she indicated that she'd taken his suspicions seriously. She hadn't mocked like Merchant, but she had shown exasperation; grown angry. And if that had been her way of trying to head him off it was too oblique to have succeeded.

If—as now seemed clear—she was more informed than he could have been expected to believe then, surely, she ought to have told him; warned him openly. Vega—Merchant—Los Colmillos. . . . Perversely, he wanted more than a few hasty lines. The wounds were slow to heal and he was still baffled. *Frank's going to sort out the mess. Do as he says, exactly as he says* . . . How close were they, those two?

He went back into the auditorium and rejoined Lloyd.

"All right?"

Brennan tilted his head grudgingly. It was easy to be ungrateful. "How long do we stay here?"

"Till about sundown."

He groaned.

"Merchant's given me a rendezvous."

"What about the boat you were going to lay on?"

"No need now."

The woman in front shifted irritably. They broke off and stared at the screen. It was impossible to talk at any length or above a whisper. Brennan had to be content with snippets.

"Eleven o'clock . . . Espada Point—beyond Monterrey . . . Getaway crew provided . . . Sudden anxiety on everyone's part to come to your aid. Marvellous, eh . . ."

It wouldn't be dark until six or more. Brennan shut his eyes, memories and uncertainty crowding in. *Dearest Harry* . . . The exact wording of Alison's note he could no longer recollect, but this clung like a burr.

"Will I see her?" He sounded like a prisoner: plans were so vague.

"God knows, chum. It's Merchant's show."

Lloyd sat with the camera and flash attachment cased on his lap. When he breathed into Brennan's ear his voice was as jaunty as ever, but when the house-lights eventually swelled again Brennan noticed the tell-tale movements of his hands and the nervous tic which occasionally flicked at his mouth. The camera-straps were twisted as tight as a plait.

"You aren't still going to try it, surely?"

"I'd never forgive myself if I didn't."

"You're crazy."

136

"So you said before."

"*And* make the rendezvous?"

"D.V."

"We aren't the only ones in the know—it's beginning to stick out a mile. Why risk your neck when official confirmation's for the asking?"

Lloyd made no reply.

"You've got your story." Brennan urged. "Why else am I on the run? Why else was Vega arrested? Why else should Merchant—and Cooper—be so ready to smuggle me away? They must have all the proof that's going."

"I doubt it."

"It stands to reason."

"López continues to occupy the Palace, chum, and tonight he's throwing a party. They can't have enough to jump him yet, otherwise it wouldn't be so. And I'm not waiting around for someone to pounce. I'm coming out with you at eleven with something better than official confirmation, so help me."

A man struggled along the row. While the interval lasted they could talk more freely, but soon they were subjected to the saccharine charms of Hawaii; reduced to spasmodic exchanges. Lloyd's determination amazed Brennan. His own predicament was comparatively simple. The wider issues had never been in business. The two-jawed vice of inhibiting force and deceitful propaganda which gripped Santa Marta was there for those who looked for it. That López had come to power after half a dozen bloody changes of government and a parody of an election was for the historians; and if he were about to be tumbled from his Presidential chair that was for the professionals to handle. For Brennan, the thought of Alison outweighed the high drama. Events had trapped him, but they set no challenge. Suspicion, shock, fear—all these had been his: but he was spared having to prove himself. Courage could be a difficult neurosis and when he glanced at Lloyd it was with pity and alarm—as well as with irritation that a man's fixation could so endanger the plans of others.

Leaning close, whispering again, he said: "Between leaving here and eleven o'clock—"

"Yes?"

"What the devil am I supposed to do with myself?"

"There'll be time to think about that."

"When, for Pete's sake?" He was sick of being handled like a package. There had been too much evasiveness; too much held back. From the moment Alison denounced him he seemed to have been deprived of his identity. "Let's talk about it now."

The woman in front hissed at them again and her neighbour swore: "*Madre de Dios!*" An attendant waggled a torch in their direction.

"Later," Lloyd breathed.

"Now," Brennan insisted, provoked.

"Hold your horses, chum."

"Now. Come on."

He stood up. With some reluctance Lloyd, who was on the outside, rose too. Brennan followed him down the shallow stairs. "Hawaii," a nasal voice disclaimed. "Hawaii, where your house-boy wakes you with the words: 'The sun is one palm tree high' . . ." Lloyd elbowed through the doors under the CABAL-LEROS sign, Brennan on his heels. No one was there.

"Well?"

"Well, what?"

"I'm not exactly armed to the teeth with information, am I?"

"Merchant didn't give me a printed hand-out, you know. We're to be at Espada Point at eleven o'clock. That's all there is to it."

"Am I supposed to take a taxi?"

"Of course not."

"How do I get there, then? I don't know Espada Point from Timbuctoo."

"My car's rented, so it's expendable. We use that."

"But you're going to be otherwise engaged."

"Not for long." Lloyd licked his lips. "Not for too long."

"What happens if you come unstuck?"

"Then—in a manner of speaking—the car's all yours." His smile was a disaster.

"You want me to wait in it—is that it?"

"Yes and no."

138

Brennan frowned. "I don't get you."

"Look," Lloyd began awkwardly, then stopped as the automatic cistern flushed.

"Go on."

"It's not easy." He flicked his lighter and lit a cigarette. The travelogue commentary was muffled, as if the voice were straining through a gag. "Asking a favour is never easy, and this one's like going down on my knees."

"Favour?"

With difficulty Lloyd held Brennan's gaze. "Chum," he said. "I'll fluff it on my own. You bet."

"Then cut it out."

"I can't."

"For the sake of a blasted newspaper?"

Lloyd shook his head. "That's only part of the battle. I told you: it gets harder. Every time it comes to the pinch it gets harder." He made an intense gesture. "You won't understand, but take it from me it can happen to a man. I'm scared right down to the rivets, that's the truth. There's a thread or two holding together, not much more, and I almost wish they'd gone, too. Then I'd be spared this. I could say 'To blazes' and only have to start trying to learn to live with myself. But that hasn't happened yet."

It astonished Brennan that someone could so bare himself and yet retain a shred of dignity. "What are you expecting me to do?"

"Lend a hand."

"Hold yours, you mean."

Lloyd's mouth twitched. "*Touché*. But you're wrong."

The door was flung open, and Brennan started, nerves shaming his last remark. Two youths crowded in, jabbering excitedly. Lloyd made a pretence of washing: Brennan fumbled for cigarettes and lit up, his back to the cubicles. It seemed a long time before he and Lloyd were alone again.

"You're wrong, chum," Lloyd repeated, mouth askew. "If it were that bad I'd have tried to hold you to ransom by keeping the R.V. to myself. But if I go and balls-up the photographs I'll kick myself from here to kingdom come. I'd have been on the high wire for nothing, and I'll never make it again."

Brennan stared at him. "You want me *in* there?"

"Who better?"

"You couldn't make a mistake with the Yashica even if you tried. It's foolproof."

"But *I'm* not. I've never got beyond 'Watch the birdie'."

The electric-guitars were sobbing faintly through the walls. Brennan turned from Lloyd as if to escape the pressure of what he was asking. There couldn't have been a worse time to be indebted to anyone. He owed him something. Even so, he continued to ward him off.

"You aren't even sure the morgue will turn out to be the right place."

"That's a chance I must take."

"How d'you propose getting in?"

"Any old way except via the front door."

"And then?"

"I've a rough idea of the layout."

Brennan glanced at Lloyd's reflection in the mirror. "It'll be madness. Plain bloody madness." He shook his head with finality, yet he could feel his resolve beginning to buckle under the great weight of the silence that followed. *Do as Frank says, exactly as he says, and everything will be all right* . . . Once again he was being dragged two ways. Nothing would deter Lloyd, but his kind of desperation was the worst of goads. Bitterly, grudgingly, Brennan acknowledged his debt, yet it was concern with what Lloyd might let loose if he were unaccompanied that pulled the heavier. More than a personal grand finale was at stake. Lloyd hadn't the stamina if it came to an interrogation under a harsh light with the threat of water and rubber tubing. The Espada Point rendezvous would be in jeopardy if he operated alone—and Alison might be there.

Would be, surely? *Must* be . . .

"There's something else," Lloyd was saying.

"Tell me."

"This fellow who was stuck up in the *ceiba*—"

"Yes?"

"There'll be a choice of subject in there—road accidents, suicides . . . I haven't a clue what your Mr. X looks like. Not an inkling." Lloyd paused. "But you have, chum. You're the only one who has."

"That doesn't twist my arm one bit."

"What will, then?" He came closer, and close-to his face was lined; damp. In an entirely different voice, drained of false heroics, he said "What will?"

It was cruel to keep him in suspense; a keyhole business to watch the betraying tic that escaped control.

"Nothing," Brennan said. Yet he added: "But I'll come if I must." And even as he made the decision he knew that he was going to miss the comforting feel of his gun.

CHAPTER TWELVE

THEY sat through the Cary Grant picture one more time, but they were spared Hawaii. The clock was showing after six by the time the interval came round and Lloyd nudged Brennan in the ribs. After almost five hours of near darkness and comparative security the neon-lit foyer seemed to Brennan dangerously bright, and the ebb and flow of crowds in the murky street released the hunted feeling into his system. There were too many uniforms about for comfort.

"Where's the car?"

"Round the next corner."

Dusk was thickening fast. The sky was clouded over and a breeze moved the shadowy tulip trees in the park opposite; showered pollen from the planes lining the roadway. They walked the length of the block together. A gritty dust-devil twirled across their path as they reached the intersection and Brennan screwed his eyes. When he opened them again he found that Lloyd had stopped. There was a parking sign at the head of the side street and Lloyd's car was about the fourth along.

"Police," Lloyd said out of the corner of his mouth.

Only then did Brennan see the man's helmet. He was stooping to examine the rear of the car in front of Lloyd's—a battered old Chevrolet roadster. To turn away would be to invite suspicion, yet every nerve, every muscle, in Brennan's body was for doing so. But Lloyd ended his indecision by advancing again, suddenly garrulous, enthusing about the picture. As they drew level the policeman raised his head. Lloyd was between him and Brennan, but it was on Brennan that his gaze fell. Narrow features, simian eye-sockets—Brennan felt himself mesmerised and could hardly believe that the rueful smile was harmless.

To Brennan's dismay Lloyd did not pass. "What's the trouble, *amigo?*"

"A flat, señor. How d'you like that?" Apparently the car was his. "Just as I go off duty, too." He grimaced, straightening up.

"Got a pump?"

"No." He looked from one to the other, engrossed in his own misfortune. "Perhaps you, señor, are better placed? If I could borrow—"

"Sorry, but I'm not. I'll tell the service-station on the Calle Velasquez if you like. I'm going in that direction."

"It would be appreciated. Greatly appreciated."

Brennan thought Lloyd would never unlock the doors. The policeman saluted as they slammed themselves in; delayed an oncoming vehicle so that they could move out from the kerb, gratitude in every pantomimic gesture. They pulled clear and accelerated away, neither speaking. After a few hundred yards Lloyd managed a laugh. "When in doubt, chum, join 'em"; and though the laugh was shaky Brennan experienced something he never imagined he would—a touch of admiration for him. Down to his last few threads Lloyd might be; past it; over the hill. But at least he was honest and made no bones about what the effort had cost him—arming sweat from his face, unashamedly incapable of putting a cigarette between his lips, let alone lighting it.

"Do it for me, will you, chum? I've got St. Vitus's Dance."

Brennan lit two; handed one across. Lloyd nodded. They were heading towards the Avenida del Conquistador, relatively safe, anonymous, one car amongst a stream of others. Soon they were cruising past the Palace. The floodlighting gave it a curiously two-dimensional look, like a painted cut-out. The gaudy Presidential flag was flicking horizontally and Lloyd jerked: "How's your *mal de mer*?"

"Fair."

"More than mine is. There's quite a blow coming on."

"I'll worry about that when I have to." Sightseers were already gathering at the Palace gates. "What time's the Reception?" Alison was inescapable.

"Eightish. I've a ticket somewhere. How's that for a joke?" Lloyd laughed again, hunched behind the wheel. A spitting tram lurched alongside as he slowed at a red light and swarthy faces stared morosely down at them. "Little do they know," Lloyd muttered. "Just look at the poor bastards." Nerves were forcing him to talk. "Average expectation of life forty years. Solaces—religion, rum and cock-fights. Fears—hunger, disease and jail. When Lôpez took over his slogan was: We must dignify human beings. And the Americans fell for it." He tossed his glowing butt away and went clumsily into gear. "Poor sods, each and every one, with never a chance."

A fountain sparkled at the hub of a roundabout. La Granja market was somewhere off right; the Oasis Club two blocks and a turn to the left. Familiar ground prompted the thought of Alison again; Merchant, too . . . Brennan shifted position, trying not to imagine her amazed eyes if she could see him now and know where he was bound—in apparent defiance of her and all common sense. He had eaten only a light breakfast and no lunch, yet he wasn't hungry. His stomach seemed to have shrunk to nothing and his palms were unnaturally moist. He was committed, and for a reason, but Lloyd's was a private war.

"How far now?"

"A couple of minutes."

Darkness had come right down. Away from the glitter of the main thoroughfares the street-lamps were dim and widely spaced, but Lloyd made do with his sidelights. The gutted stalls of La Granja market formed an inner square to the plaza of the same name. Row upon row of broken and twisted structures filled the central area. Some days earlier Brennan had wandered along the crowded dividing lanes and marvelled at the colours—not only of the piled fruit but of the dresses and skins of the women who bought and sold. It was a hubbub then, but now it was abandoned. The lanes hadn't even been swept clear. Lloyd brought the car to a halt and switched off. A charred smell flooded in. A cat, hideously skinny, prowled amongst the shadows.

"Which way from here?"

Lloyd used his head. "See the street leading out? Say a hundred and fifty yards along to the left. It's set back a bit. There are railings all round, then a strip of grass, then a gravel path close to the walls."

Brennan said nothing. Somewhere in his mind he had begun to nourish the hope that they would fail to get inside. He reached over to the back seat and lifted the Yashica; eased it from its case. Holding it close to the facia-panel he familiarised himself with the mechanism and made a few imaginary exposures. The film Lloyd had brought was Ilford HP3—fast enough. Brennan fixed a setting of f 22 and a sixtieth. Then he clipped on the reflector and gave the battery-operated flash a trial. There was a crinkling sound as the bulb fired. For a split second every detail of Lloyd's pallid face was revealed by the leaping, stark white brightness, and he flinched from it, hands flying up.

There were eleven more bulbs in the pack. Brennan screwed in a new one and dropped the rest into his breast pocket. Finally he loaded the film and wound it on, inevitably reminded of Vega and the early lies, the last time he had held a camera, the very beginnings of all this. Lloyd hadn't existed then. Yet here he was saying: "Satisfied?"

"It's okay. . . . How's the time?"

"Quarter to seven."

Neither moved. Then Brennan complained: "What d'you expect to find?—an open window?" They had no plans; no plans at all. It was imbecilic. But the way his heart-beat was beginning to quicken was the measure of reality. "And what happens if there's a hullaballoo? Say we're separated?"

Lloyd's answer was to hand him a spare car-key. "First come, first served." He resorted to melodrama as if it were a drug.

"That's not good enough."

"What more d'you want?"

"An intermediate rendezvous."

"Where?"

"Say the clock-tower on the quay—any time up to nine. You know where I mean?—near *The Conch Shell*."

"Very well."

"And don't leave the car here. It's too damned conspicuous."

"I wasn't going to." Lloyd pressed the starter and nosed off the carriageway, scraping into a gap between the skeletons of two stalls. The cat mewed as the engine died. "How's that?"

"Better."

"Anything else?"

"Only," Brennan said, "that I must be clean out of my mind."

He opened the door without another word and squeezed crab-wise round to the rear of the car, burnt planking crunching underfoot. Lloyd joined him and slid a sheet of corrugated iron across the gap. The noise seemed enormous, but by the time he had finished no one from ten paces away could have suspected a vehicle was there. They turned towards the street which would lead them to the morgue, nerves hard-held, Lloyd's voice already low.

"We can get through to the side of the building along a sort of alley. I'll show you."

Brennan let him lead. The street was the Calle Doran: it was strange how minor details registered. Clustered, shabby houses of crushed coral walled it in. A few lights showed but mostly the windows were shuttered over, as though the district demanded a state of permanent mourning. There were posts at the entrance to the alley in order to restrict its use to pedestrians and a drainage rut ran along its centre. The sound of their footfalls reverberated in the narrow passage as if they were followed. After about forty yards the alley made a sharp right turn. A street-lamp showed where it ended, but obliterated what lay beyond. From somewhere in one of the darkened houses a baby wailed, and the thin, high voicing of ancestral fear tightened

Brennan's scalp. Lloyd was on the balls of his feet now, one shoulder brushing the alley's leprous stone. After a few yards more he stopped and jabbed a finger. His face was smeared with ash from the market: that, and the yellow lamp-glimmer, gave him a slightly wild appearance.

"Over there."

Brennan nodded. The quiet was uncanny. A lorry rattled in the near distance. They passed quickly under the lamp, debouching into another street which, farther down, made a T-junction with the Calle Doran. As their shadows sprouted ahead of them Brennan saw the railings Lloyd had mentioned and the squat bulk of the morgue. It was smaller than he had expected, cheese-coloured, with a flat roof and regularly-spaced windows—about eight, he thought; all unlit. The gates and entrance were to their right, hidden from them. The guard was somewhere there. Instinctively they veered left, undisturbed still, the night to themselves. It was early for lovers and nobody strolled or gossiped. La Paz tinted the dragging clouds. The city seemed remote, but tension provided continuity. Midway between two lamps Lloyd paused, looked round, then began to clamber over the railings. They were chest high, topped with blunt spikes; almost too much for him. Wheezing, he dropped heavily on to the grass. Brennan passed him the camera before heaving himself across: it wasn't easy and he tried to shut his mind to what might happen if there was an alarm and they had to run. The strip of grass was some twenty-five feet wide. They covered it like infantry nervously seeking fresh cover, inclined to stoop, knees a little bent. As they reached the gravel surround an owl flew over and the soft sigh of its wings startled them. On tiptoe they reached the building and leaned against it, pulses thudding. A cyclist was peddling along the street and they watched him uneasily, aware of the paleness of the wall behind them. When he had gone by Brennan brought his head to within inches of Lloyd's.

"Bars." He raised his eyes, unable to disguise his satisfaction. A mesh of iron, cemented into the stone, criss-crossed each window. And the windows were small and high, the weathered

146

sills at least ten feet from the ground. "You'll never get past those."

Lloyd pursed his lips, staring up. He was sweating profusely and the smears of ash had run together.

"Impossible," Brennan muttered almost inaudibly.

". . . try the back."

"It'll be the same there."

Lloyd was too intent to listen. "Come on."

They avoided the gravel and moved furtively along the edge of the grass. The morgue was rectangular, structurally without frills, its rear a narrow replica of what they had already seen—the sealed windows beyond reach and solidly barred. Brennan's hope gained ground.

"No use," he breathed again, but Lloyd was making for the far corner. Brennan shifted his hold on the camera and turned at the angle of grass, expecting to find the same impregnable length of stone and grilled windows. But he was wrong: Lloyd had stopped opposite an iron-studded door and was beckoning.

Even then Brennan banked on it being locked. Together they stepped cautiously on to the gravel, theirs the only sounds. There was an iron ring for a handle and Lloyd reached for it, fingers trembling. He wasn't sparing himself. The ring moved but the door did not. Using a shoulder Lloyd tried again, lips parted, increasing the pressure as carefully as a cracksmith. Seconds elapsed, but nothing happened.

"Leave it," Brennan started to say, when suddenly, with a dry groan, the door yielded. Off-balance, Lloyd almost stumbled but managed to check the door from opening more than a few inches. A black, vertical slit was all that showed. They waited, listening. At last, with an ambivalent glance at Brennan, elated yet fearful, Lloyd opened the door a shade wider and stepped inside. Brennan followed and found himself wrapped in darkness. The air was cellar cool; everything eerily still. For perhaps half a minute neither moved, tense, ears straining. Then, gently, Brennan swung the door to without engaging the catch. Lloyd got his lighter to work and held the tiny flame head high. They were in a bare corridor leading towards some stone steps. On one wall was a battery of fuse-boxes; on the floor against the other a couple of wooden trestles and some worn brooms.

The slightest noise seemed to be magnified out of all proportion—Lloyd's breathing, the merest scrape of shoes, a knee-joint cracking . . . There were eight steps, and Brennan kept close on Lloyd's heels. They had just reached the new level when, without warning, a deep humming began. Lloyd's body jerked visibly and a strangled "Aaaaah" escaped him. The lighter fell from his raised hand and snapped out; bounced somewhere across the corridor before coming to rest. The humming went on, seeming to come from all sides at once. The short hairs on Brennan's neck bristled. He was shaken as much by Lloyd's reaction as anything. But reason eventually prevailed. "Dynamo?"

"Refrigeration plant." For someone whose veneer was so dangerously thin Lloyd had recovered well. "That'll be it." Then: "Where's that bloody lighter?"

"Hang on."

Fumbling, Brennan managed to strike a match. Lloyd retrieved the lighter and flicked it into life. Five yards from where they stood the corridor turned left. They made progress again, their shadows grotesquely deformed, minor sounds deadened by the continuing low-pitched hum. There were no windows. After rounding the turn they found themselves level with a plain wooden door. Maintenance staff only . . . The humming was more concentrated here, its point of origin more certain. Lloyd tried the door, but it wouldn't budge. He gestured, indicating that it didn't matter, and led on. Now there were two steps down, after which the corridor again changed direction—right this time. Some fire-buckets filled with sand were hung on pegs at the corner. As Lloyd reached these he suddenly extinguished the lighter and Brennan cannoned into him. In the same moment, with unnerving clarity, he heard a man cough.

He went rigid, pressed against the wall. The cough had sounded incredibly close and he was aware that the darkness wasn't quite as intense as before. Lloyd's wispy hair brushed against his face.

"There's a room—"

"Where?"

"A few yards."

Brennan craned his head past Lloyd's and peered round the end bucket. A bar of light fell into the corridor from a slightly open door on the left-hand side. If he had been alone he would have retreated there and then, but to his utter consternation Lloyd recklessly edged forward. He tried to check him but it was impossible. Fool, his mind hammered. *Fool* . . . Yet he followed, sweating ice and fire, alarm sweeping anger aside. To the door was about seven or eight desperately careful toe-pointed paces. Whoever was in the room coughed a second time when they were half-way towards it and there was a crisp rustle of a newspaper being folded. The door was barely ajar. Through the hinge-crack Brennan glimpsed a man in shirt-sleeves seated at a table, a bottle, a peaked cap, a propped rifle . . . It seemed impossible that they would get by without being heard or without the man chancing to come out to stretch his legs. And they would have to run the risk a second time: every step would have to be retraced. Brennan experienced no relief as they crept clear. An error now, and they were trapped. And for what? For what?

The next few minutes were the longest of his life. Neither of them dared make a light and they felt their way a few inches at a time. For what seemed an endless distance there were no more turns, nothing to shield them from discovery, and never a second passed without Brennan expecting a challenge from behind. Either he bumped into Lloyd or he lost contact with him. Then, just when he had begun to think it would never happen, the corridor changed direction and he risked the splutter of a match. Immediately in front of them was another door, of steel, with a slim lever-and-socket handle and rubber-sealed edges. ENTRADA PROHIBIDA. He peered at Lloyd as the match died and Lloyd nodded, skin drenched, mouth loose— nodded as if to say: "This is it."

There was a faint vacuum-release *fuff* as the door opened. Once again they stepped into a dark void, but there were windows to give vague shape and dimension to their whereabouts. Very softly the humming was here, too, and the air was considerably cooler. Lloyd pushed the lever home, sealing them in, and they waited, giving their eyes time. It was several moments before Brennan realised that he was on a landing at the top of a short staircase: perhaps half a dozen steps descended between metal railings. To either side, beneath the windows, he saw what looked like a row of large filing-cabinets. They were painted white and he guessed what they were.

Lloyd touched him on the arm. "Front of the building's straight ahead—officers, admin." His teeth were beginning to chatter as if he had all but spent himself again. "Let's get down." The place was like a whispering gallery.

Brennan went first. The floor was tiled and as smooth as glass. He had the feeling that they were a little below ground-level. He waited for Lloyd to join him, and Lloyd breathed: "Start at this end."

The cabinets were aligned like washing-machines in a launder-ette, but closer together, oval-topped and about five feet in height. Lloyd moved quietly to the nearest one and opened it. Inside were two drawers, double-banked, with frontal identification-cards. Lloyd flicked his lighter. The cards were blank, but even so he pulled the drawers. They ran easily, with scarcely a sound, and each time Brennan found himself staring into an empty, glistening compartment. They went to the second cabinet, but that was also empty. So were the third and fourth. They worked methodically along the line. Once, a sickly-sweet smell wafted up as a drawer slid out, but the drawer itself was vacant like the others.

Brennan's nerves were too frayed for him to be squeamish. "And when they got there the cupboard was bare." He muttered it with anger, suddenly incensed that he should be risking so much on the strength of another of Lloyd's hunches. There was a guard—yes: but what did that signify? A guard was probably routine. Eight or nine cabinets checked and not a single body, let alone the one they sought. A camera had never seemed so futile a piece of equiment.

There were a dozen cabinets in the row and they had reached two from the end before any of the cards were written on. Scrawled in violet ink was *Rio Amarillo*. The date was the previous day's and rubber-stamped. Lloyd hesitated for a moment, his Adam's-apple bouncing, before opening the drawer and lifting the limp cold cloth. Whoever the woman was she looked tranquil enough and Lloyd pushed her carefully back like a tray of ice-cubes. Simultaneously, as the drawer padded home, the humming stopped and total silence enveloped them—so intense that for a few seconds they were shocked into immobility. The grave would be like this. Then, outside, an owl screeched and they moved again as if released by a signal, caution redoubled.

Both cards in the last cabinet bore the same record—*Avenida de los Limeros*, after which, bracketed in a different coloured ink, was *Camión*. Lloyd checked each drawer and Brennan wished that he hadn't. A man first, then a boy—at least, he supposed it was a boy. He shut his eyes before the wavering light went out, sickened, callousness sloughing off.

"Other side." This was Lloyd, half his hopes gone, sustained by the gamble of what awaited them. His expression was feverish as he brought the lighter into play at the first of the new batch of cabinets. The drawers slid forward, slowly revealing their contents. A negro with a dancer's head and torn throat; a wasted young girl. A bead of Lloyd's sweat fell on to her temple and the tiny plop was like that of a living thing. The flame trembled. Lloyd gulped audibly and shoved her gently where she belonged.

On and off the lighter went as the cabinets were opened, the stem of flame beginning to shrink. *Calle Cuervo*, the cards read; *Puerto La Paz, Los Tres Cignes (Taberna, Calle Barandilla)* . . . There were always dates but never a name. The lost and the found. Once there was merely a query. A sense of nightmare began to overtake Brennan. He hadn't bargained for this. He had an almost hysterical urge to look no more, to quit, to get clear while they could and escape the claustrophobic silence and cool, sterile air.

There were five more cabinets. The first was unoccupied, the second contained a newly-born child, huddled as if still in the womb. *La Catedral* . . . Then there was a grown man, as pale as alabaster, with a stubble of hair blueing the square jaw. Brennan's glance was cursory, but Lloyd kept the drawer extended.

"Mean anything?"

"No." The whisper's echo fluttered. "Why should it?"

"There's nothing on the card."

Brennan forced himself to look again. "No."

Lloyd bit his lips. They moved along. Again the cards were blank, but the drawers were not. When Lloyd lifted the first cloth Brennan felt a squirm of revulsion, yet the features were destroyed in such a way as to seem hideously familiar. He hesitated, but Lloyd muttered: "No use," and stooped for the lower compartment. It rattled slightly as he dragged it out. Lighter held high he peeled back the cloth. Brennan's eyes widened as the throb of recognition swept through him. The podgy face was as peaceful now as when he had last seen it high in the *ceiba*. The cropped hair, the heavy brows . . . Only the curious mottling was new.

"Yes?"

"Yes," he said.

"God . . ." Then: "You've got to be sure. One hundred per cent sure."

"I'm sure, all right."

A succession of tics twisted Lloyd's mouth. "Glory, glory Hallelujah"—he breathed it like a prayer and the ceiling echoed it back. "Now get him for me. For God's sake, get him."

Brennan raised the camera, looking fixedly at the stranger whose death had put an end to normality. The settings were already made, but he had to focus and the angle was difficult. He stood on tiptoe and leaned across the drawer, framing the face in the view-finder, instructing Lloyd to hold the lighter lower and farther back. By an effort he could discipline his mind, but his hands didn't seem to belong to him. Twice he stood away, blinking sweat from his eyes. The third time, breath held, he achieved a degree of steadiness and made the exposure. The flash lit the room like a sheet of lightning, flinging shadows against walls and windows. Then the image of the face beneath him was floating like a blurred white print on the darkness and Lloyd was asking: "Okay?"

Brennan nodded. He changed the bulb. Lloyd clicked on his sinking flame and Brennan hitched himself into position, sucking in air. The bulb spat and the flash leapt. He worked quickly yet with care. Again—now . . . The reversed image lingered less and less, as if he were laying a ghost. He took five, then cocked his head.

"Enough?"

"That's up to you."

"I'm satisfied."

Lloyd bent to shove the drawer. His teeth were chattering again, but if it was with relief it was premature. The corridor awaited them yet.

"Take it easy," Brennan warned as the drawer thudded. They turned towards the staircase.

"Mission completed." Lloyd's tone of voice indicated that he was desperately seeking refuge from himself. "And nobody had to say 'Cheese'."

The words were barely out of his mouth when a door opened behind them and all the lights were suddenly switched on.

"Who are you?"

Frozen between strides they stared unbelievingly at the soldier framed in the doorway.

"What are you doing here?" He thrust his carbine forward as if there were a bayonet on it. "Who are—"

The paralysing crescendo of dismay snapped first in Brennan, yet Lloyd beat him to the staircase. They went in a demented scramble up the short flight, and if anything saved them it was because the guard wasted precious seconds raising the alarm before opening fire. He managed only one shot before Lloyd lugged the door open, and that struck somewhere above their heads, showering plaster. They went pell-mell along the dark corridor, half-blind, crashing from wall to wall. The man on duty in the side room emerged and made a bewildered attempt to block their path, only to be knocked flying by Lloyd's butting charge. Right, then left, then right again. All the buckets came down. The corridor thudded with the sound of pursuit. Near the exit Brennan swept the brooms and trestles into a heap then jinked outside, fear yapping at his heels.

As they sprinted for the railing Lloyd was labouring. Shouting started off to their left and several figures rounded the corner from the front of the morgue, heading diagonally across the grass. Brennan threw the camera into the street and frantically started helping Lloyd past the spikes, shouldering him up like a sack. The nearest of the guards was about thirty yards away when Brennan heaved himself over. Another shot rang out, then another. He flinched instinctively, grabbing for the camera. Even then he thought they were going to make it, but Lloyd landed in a heap beside him and didn't move. For the minutest fraction of time Brennan thought that he must have winded himself.

"Lloyd!" he bawled.

Then he saw the blood. With an enormous effort he scooped Lloyd off the sidewalk and got him across his shoulders. Staggering, he made for the alley beyond the lamp, and why he wasn't hit he couldn't imagine.

CHAPTER THIRTEEN

THE alley seemed everlasting. He stumbled along it as if he were possessed, in the grip of a terror that made light of Lloyd's weight. An early ricochet shattered the lamp and the firing died, but the pursuit came on, pounding into the alley before he reached the Calle Doran. A whistle had begun to sound repeatedly but its shrill note reached Brennan without edge, blurred, as if there were shells against his ears. He slithered at the corner into the street and lurched towards the market square, canted forward, lungs burning, drums and trumpets inside his skull. For a few lifelong seconds he had the street to himself. Then there was a clatter of boots, a hoarse cry, a hollow crack, a whining eruption of stone within inches of his feet. He lowered his head and forced himself towards La Granja, hope all but gone, wincing in anticipation of the bullet that would smash him down. But the shooting was as wild as before and he gained precious yards. By the time he was in amongst the charred remains of the darkened market the nearest guards were in the

Calle Doran. He staggered to where the car was and saw two of them sprint heavily into the square, hesitate, then move different ways, like dogs suddenly deprived of a scent.

He was shaking so violently that his fingers seemed incapable of using the key once he got it out. Now there were three or four soldiers within forty paces of him, calling to each other, temporarily defeated, beginning to prowl. At most he had only a few moments. He somehow got the key into the lock and kneed the door open. Lloyd was hanging down his back like a slaughtered animal. Crouching, he lowered him roughly across the bench-seat. Then his strength gave way and he fell in on top of him, the camera clattering to the floor. There was a yell and one of the guards came breasting past the skeleton of a stall only a lane away from where the car was hidden. With a convulsive jerk Brennan disentangled his legs from Lloyd's and got himself into an upright position, simultaneously jabbing the starter. As the engine roared he flicked on the headlights. The oncoming guard recoiled, then jumped sideways as Brennan slammed in the gear and the car leapt forward. It ploughed through the wreck of stall after stall, practically out of control, the wheel spinning in Brennan's hands. The headlights picked out a couple of guards, one with rifle aimed, but if there were any shots Brennan didn't hear them. All the din in the world seemed to be concentrated within the car. Dust and debris spattered the windscreen. Lloyd's legs were still partly in the way and he shoved them brutally aside; jarred into something unseen, spun, straightened, found a lane and hurtled towards the far end of the square, the stamp of nightmare once more on his senses.

The tyres screamed as he swerved into the roadway. He snapped on the wipers and accelerated recklessly, the square vanishing in a smear of speed. A narrow street led them away— which it was and where it went he had no idea. Soon another offered itself and he followed it, slowing a little only as the sidewalks began to be populated. His mind was in appalled confusion, the numbness thawing out, bewilderment and nausea competing for possession.

"Lloyd?" he said.

There was no response. Lloyd was half on, half off, the seat.

As revealed by the passing street-lamps his smudged, upturned face had the pallor of death.

"Lloyd?"

He dared not stop, yet soon he must. Two worlds were overlapping, but the feeling of nightmare persisted—even in the laughing squeal of a girl with a tall heel trapped in a grating. He managed an ice-cold moment of sense and turned when he reached an intersection he recognised, heading south to the quays, fumbling under Lloyd's blood-soaked shirt. The heartbeat was strong though very fast. Brennan wasn't conscious of relief that it existed at all; the flow of blood was frightening. The wound seemed to be in the right of Lloyd's chest, but it was impossible to be sure. He drove towards the quays, trying desperately not to yield to panic. There was a raincoat in the back of the car and he dragged it over; covered all but Lloyd's face. Whenever the traffic slowed he suspected the worst, incapable of reasoning that it was too soon for check-points. His muscles were still shaking and his head echoed with the thud and crack of pursuit. Minutes had elapsed, minutes only, yet all sense of time had been destroyed and he visualised the hunt already narrowed down, the squads positioned.

A flashing sign directed him—THE CONCH SHELL: 200 METRES. He left the main thoroughfare and made towards the cobbled quayside, as scared and distrustful of the quiet as he'd been of the traffic-herds. Lloyd groaned as the car rattled over the cobbles. Brennan ran it into a space between others near the clock-tower and cut the engine. Music drifted out from the restaurants across the way. With a feeling of disbelief he saw that the clock was showing ten past eight.

Lloyd groaned again as Brennan began to tend him. The wound was well below the collar-bone and the bullet had drilled right through. In one of Lloyd's pockets he found a handkerchief and made a pad; tore what he could from Lloyd's shirt and his own and tried to effect a bandage. The result was crude and inadequate, but it helped to staunch the blood: offered a breathing-space in which to work out what to do next. It was futile to think of the rendezvous at Espada Point when Lloyd might

156

pump to death within an hour, yet to call at a hospital or on a doctor would be tantamount to giving themselves up.

Lloyd's eyes suddenly fluttered open. "Chum," he said weakly.

"How d'you feel?"

"Lousy. What ... what happened?"

"We almost got away with it, that's what happened."

"Where are we?"

"By *The Conch Shell*."

Lloyd winced, fingers exploring the area of the wound. "Shoulder, is it?" Beneath the daubs of ash his face had gone a dreadful green colour.

Brennan nodded. "You need a doctor."

"What's the time?"

"Eight fifteen."

"I'll manage ... without one, thanks. Must."

"You've lost a whole lot of blood. You'll never—"

Lloyd stiffened, eyes widening as if he had just remembered the crux of a dream. "What about the camera?"

"It's here."

"Intact?"

"Yes."

He shuddered a sigh. "You're a marvel, chum. God, you are." There was silence for a moment, and when he spoke again it was from the back of his throat. "Don't ruin everything, whatever you do. I'll ... make out."

"Sure you will, but —"

"It'd be as good as turning me in."

"Look," Brennan said, clutching at a straw. "We could go back to the Casa Abril—"

"Never."

"She'd let you lie up for a while."

Lloyd rolled his head on the seat. "She'd see us hanged first."

"I'll ring Cooper, then."

"The line'll be tapped. They'd ... they'd get to us before anyone from the Embassy did. And don't ... go near the Embassy either. ... Any case, Cooper won't be there. Not ... tonight. He'll be at the Palace. All the world and his wife—"

The whisper petered out and he lay quite still. Brennan had never felt more alone, his despair more complete, more lasting, than anything he had ever before experienced. All power of decision had been sapped away and he put his head in his hands, trembling, telling himself that they would have been spared disaster if he had managed to dissuade Lloyd in the first place— forgetting that no one could have done that, forgetting too that by joining him he had vaguely hoped to safeguard the rendezvous by bolstering Lloyd's nerve.

Voices presently alerted him. A man and woman were leaving the bar next to *The Conch Shell*. They were formally dressed and the saloon they entered bore a CD plate: Brennan could imagine their destination. A trick of light, and the man's build, reminded him forcibly of Cooper. Impetuously he leaned across and wound the near-side window down, only to realise that he was mistaken. Almost with hate he watched the saloon recede, then turned his attention back to Lloyd.

Mother of God, what was best?

Lloyd's wallet had fallen on to the seat. Brennan picked it up and, as he did so, something slid to the floor. Looking to see what it was he found himself staring at an invitation to the Presidential Reception. He straightened slowly, as if experiencing a gradual electric shock, the germ of an idea taking root, as rash as any that Lloyd might have conceived yet no more desperate than their situation. He had existed for so long on a razor's edge that caution had ceased to count.

Admit One.

There was a chance this way, just a chance, perhaps the only one, and unless he took it he doubted if Lloyd would reach Espada Point alive. Cooper had to be contacted somehow—and Lloyd qualified for help even if an Irishman did not.

He allowed himself no time to reconsider. After checking Lloyd's pulse and rearranging the raincoat he took some money from the wallet. There was blood all over his own jacket. He slipped it off, then got out and locked both doors. A steady breeze blew and the dark sea was ruffled—but the sea could wait; he was chained to here and now. He walked past the clock-tower towards the queue of taxis farther down the quay, capable even then of amazement that he had so easily decided what he required. The driver at the front of the queue greeted him expectantly, but he continued until he was about six or seven vehicles along. A burly mulatto squatted on the running-board, paring his finger-nails with a clasp-knife, and he mistook the reason for Brennan's approach.

"You'll have to go to the head of the line—sorry."

"I don't want a taxi." An effort was needed. "I want to buy your coat and cap."

"Señor?"

"Your coat and cap." Far off, a siren was sounding.

The driver bared his teeth. He stood up languidly, holding the grin. "How about the car as well?" It was early for drunks. "Very cheap, señor."

"I'm serious. Just your coat and cap. I'll pay whatever you ask."

"A hundred pesos?"

"If that's what you want."

The driver blinked: one hundred pesos was a month's earnings. He looked carefully at Brennan. Dishevelled, yes. Wild-eyed, yes. But not, he thought, from liquor. "For a cap and jacket? *Señor!*" He laughed, spreading vast hands.

Brennan produced the fold of notes. "There's no catch."

"Why should they interest you? The cap is hardly new, and the jacket—"

"It's to do with a bet."

"A bet?"

"That's right."

"What kind of bet?"

"It's more of a game. . . . A treasure-hunt. I've got a list of things to collect by nine o'clock." Brennan started counting out the hundred. "What do you say?"

"Now?"

"Yes." He lied with the effortlessness of the slightly deranged. "I've also got to get a drumstick and some coconut milk and a weighing-machine ticket."

The driver laughed again. The cruise-ships brought in the

strangest people, more often as childlike as they were rich. "A hundred is impossible."

"How much, then?"

"I am not a thief, señor ... Forty, perhaps?"

"It's up to you."

The driver thumbed his thick lips. "Fifty?"

"Okay."

Brennan gave him the money. The driver peeled off the coat, waggling his head as he emptied the pockets. The craziest things happened, but this beat all. "It will never fit you. You and I aren't—"

"That won't matter."

"But it will help you to win your bet—yes?"

"I hope so."

Brennan slung the coat over his arm and took the cap. The jacket was of coarse grey hopsack; the peaked cap limp and sweaty. "Many thanks."

The driver shrugged, hugely amused. "*Adios*, señor. Good luck with the rest of the game."

He started down the line of taxis, brandishing the money, eager to tell his story; show evidence of his luck. Brennan cut away towards the clock-tower. It was exactly half past eight and he heard the banshee-wail of the siren, closer now. Lloyd was as he had left him. Brennan opened up and squeezed in behind the wheel. As he bumped along the quay the mulatto pointed him out and a knot of colleagues waved and sounded their horns. "*Suerte! . . . Que hombre! . . .*" He went to the far end of the waterfront, the deserted end, before stopping. There, as gently as he could, he dragged Lloyd into the back seat and propped him up with the raincoat buttoned round him. Lloyd moaned; muttered something. Brennan hurriedly wiped the car over, then put on the jacket and the cap. The jacket would serve as it was, but the cap was enormous: farce intruded even now. He plugged the inner rim with wads of paper tissue from the glove-pocket and fitted the cap on again. A police-wagon came screaming down to the quay at the very moment he chose to leave. It swung past within yards, close enough for Brennan to glimpse a load of armed men, but as far as he could tell he was spared their scrutiny. He drew away in the opposite direction and headed grimly into the side-streets that pointed like ribs towards the bright, wide spine of the city. Almost at once he was hailed by a woman. Her mistake was reassuring, but violence and necessity had numbed his imagination and to begin with he proceeded with a sense of inevitability, the rear-view mirror adjusted so that he could watch to see if Lloyd remained upright.

Admit One. The gilt-rimmed card lay on the ledge above the fascia-panel. *His Excellency Manuel Francisco López is pleased to anticipate your company at a Reception to be held at the Palace of the President, La Paz, on Sunday, April 21st . . .*

"Will you be there, Harry?" The sense of nightmare gradually started to tug at him again, sucking him down into a whirlpool of every freak of chance and misunderstanding that had brought him to where he was now. And in a sudden delirious release Lloyd called out: "The camera . . . You've got the camera?"—the utterance timed as if to stress that more was at stake than his own survival, more than a story, more than a rendezvous.

Brennan eyed him anxiously in the mirror. Tucked in behind them was a taxi. It came alongside at the next intersection and the man at the wheel glowered across the gap.

"Where's your disc, *amigo*?"

"*Como?*"

"Registration disc."

The morose voice was loaded with accusation. Brennan stared woodenly, his face shadowed by the cap's peak, masking alarm.

"Sodding pirates like you should be run off the road. I hope on the Holy Cross that you don't last the night."

A shift in the traffic saved Brennan from more. He escaped into the avenue and kept to the slow lane, the threat of exposure multiplying in his mind. Past the Casino, past the statue of El Conquistador; on past the first of the fountains. Another minute and he would have finally surrendered choice. Already he could see the Presidential flag tugging at its mast; already the Palace-bound cars were siphoning out of the main stream, guided by a thickening of municipal police. A swift and terrible escalation of fear almost made him turn away, but the sound of sirens checked him. What was the alternative? Where? . . . He clenched his jaws and went on, the car ready but his trust in it weakened, acutely conscious of the absence of commercial registration, wondering what else might betray them. A lanky policeman, unconcerned with such trivia, shepherded him into line as he neared the gates. Lloyd groaned loudly, but an agonised check showed that he hadn't budged. Immediately ahead of them were three other cars and Brennan edged slowly forward, wire-taut, plucking the cap farther down over his eyes. The sentry-boxes on either side of the gates were unoccupied. Tonight the Palace Guard was acting host — politely checking guests, giving instructions; already bored with raising gloved hands in salute. Four hundred cars had so far gone through. If Brennan had been able to realise this he might have been spared a fraction of what he suffered when his turn came.

"Card, please."

He handed it through the window. Every look and every gesture of the sergeant which could bring disaster landsliding down seemed to be carried through in slow motion.

"Señor Lloyd?"

Brennan grunted.

"Straight on." The breeze ruffled the fancy plumes on the preposterous helmet. "Set your passenger down at the steps, then continue as indicated."

The card was returned. The sergeant's glance into the back was as perfunctory as the accompanying salute. Brennan let in the clutch and passed through the gates, sweating coldly, in dread of a belated shout. The driveway curved towards the floodlit Palace through smooth expanses of lawn and flower-beds. The car ahead of him was about half-way to the great stone staircase that led up to the entrance terrace: others were already discharging their occupants, others drawing away. At most, Brennan had two hundred yards in which to act: the staircase was as bright and crowded as a stage. The only cover was off to the left where trees and bushes bordered the drive-way in planned disorder. With an eye on the rear-view mirror to watch how closely he was being followed in he searched frantically for a gap. Like Lloyd he had planned nothing. Nothing. His chances were rapidly whittling away when his lights revealed a path with a low, white board marked PRIVADO. It was a footpath, paved, but its trimmed edges were wide enough to take him. In an instant of decision he blacked out and wrenched the wheel over, accelerating as fast as he dared. Seconds afterwards, the car which had been behind him at the gates swept up the driveway past his bolthole.

Instinct as much as vision kept Brennan on course. It was almost impossible to see and first one wing, then the other, scraped foliage. He slowed right down and felt his way in this fashion until he thought it safe to use his sidelights. Dimly, the path led on through a mass of flowering shrubs. After a minute or so it ended in front of a hollow square of glass-houses and he turned the car on the central patch of bare earth, bringing it to rest under the lee of a laurel hedge.

Lloyd had pitched sideways on to the seat. Brennan straightened him, but made no attempt to prop him up. Carefully, he opened the door and eased himself out. Tree-frogs and cicadas were in spasmodic rivalry and he thought he could hear the strains of a military band. He took off the cap but kept the jacket on—large though it was he would be more conspicuous without it than with. Before locking the car he leaned in and finger-combed his hair in the mirror. Luck had sided with them for once, but he couldn't believe it would last and he was going to need every scrap there was to be had.

A blob of rain struck his face as he hurried away, making him start, nerves near to snapping-point. The Presidential grounds were roughly rectangular and he moved between the driveway and the high, barbed outer wall. Shadows swirled misshapenly around him as a succession of cars ran by with more late arrivals. The mincing beat of the music grew more distinct. At either side of the Palace an isthmus of grass joined the approach gardens to those at the rear. As his angle widened, Brennan saw the first of several enormous pennanted marquees and then a dais on which were stacked a score of chocolate-box bandsmen. Using what cover there was he continued until the Palace was end-on. By this time the entire party scene had come into view and every wild and ill-considered hope that had brought him there took a killing knock. With dismay he gazed at the horse-shoe of marquees and the casual mingling of a thousand guests. It would be a miracle if he even singled Cooper out, let alone made contact.

A squall of thunderdrops spattered down, too brief to produce a general surge towards the marquees but sufficient for Brennan almost to clench his fists at the sky. If any sort of hope remained it existed in the weather not driving everyone under canvas before he had at least circled the area. He kept as close to the fringes of formal lawn as he dared, oblivious of the heavy scent of roses or the flower-beds he trampled through. Squads of men were adjusting guy-ropes at the back of the marquees and the multiple skeins of coloured bulbs which spanned the alfresco heart of the proceedings were beginning to jig a shade ominously. Bright-sashed waiters threaded back and forth, and as Brennan moved so everyone also seemed to move, this way and that, to their own time, all slowly revolving around the central dais where the band churned out a muted *passacaglia* and its caparisoned conductor jerked as stiffly as a marionette.

Vainly, he looked for Cooper. Cooper was tall, florid, with crinkled hair. And slim . . . Brennan had to keep reminding himself. No moustache. Hair turning grey . . . Once, as he paused at a gap in some privet and searched among the cliques of uniformed attachés, he saw the sharp, animated features of Ricardo de Saumarez, curator of the La Paz Zoo—someone he knew, or at least had met. It would have been the easiest thing in the world to have called his name—they were that close. But Brennan drew away, backing through a cascade of weeping willows. A woman's laughter, faint yet incessant, followed him. Between marquees he glimpsed another kaleidoscope of strangers —all useless, all dangerous. Behind him as he stumbled were the roped-off rocket batteries and the intricate set-piece of the midnight fireworks display—a slatted steel frame bearing a web-like resemblance to López, below which the VIVA PAN-AMERICANO! lie was also due to flare and splutter when the hour came. The mockery of the wording was lost on Brennan. Even when he caught sight of the material López and the posse of interpreters, bodyguards and Presidential officials surrounding the small, leather-skinned man, there was no sense of irony. All he could think of was Lloyd huddled in the back of the car by the glass-houses and the need to locate Cooper.

He found a fresh place from which to crouch and peer. At least ten minutes must have slipped away since he left Lloyd. Another rattle of rain, as heavy as bird-droppings, beat through the crested heads of the royal palms under which he loitered. A warm gust plucked at the hanging lights and the trombone-player's music-sheet careered away as if attached to elastic. Some of the women pressed a protecting hand to their hair and made for the nearest refuge. God, what chance had he got? All shades of skins, all manner of gestures, builds, groupings, the collision of many tongues—his gaze flickered over the men, the hundreds of men. "You won't be missing much," Cooper had said. "I'd prefer a decent steak and a bottle of wine any day"—and the memory of his saying it came at Brennan to grind him further into hopelessness. Was Cooper here at all?

He ducked elsewhere, seeking a fresh angle, as furtive as a thief. Just in time he noticed a patrolling guard and hastily took cover, then ventured forward again. In a pause while the band changed its music he distinctly heard the wail of a siren somewhere far beyond the Palace walls. The crowds were thinning a little, filling the flapping marquees as the breeze insisted. As he watched them diminish he thought of trying to isolate a waiter and risking a bribe; persuading him to go in search of Cooper to report an accident involving the Embassy car. But when he wanted one most, none came near. Another rain-shower spat from the dragging sky. The band played on, but he noticed that the President's party was already leaving the lawn and with anguish he knew it would be a signal for everyone else to follow.

And then, with a shiver of recognition, he saw Cooper.

For the second time that night he didn't hesitate. Boldly, he stepped clear of the bushes and advanced across the grass under the swinging lights. Guests were dispersing in all directions, but the weather was suddenly his ally; scarcely a soul even glanced at him. There was a woman with Cooper, in pale blue. Brennan never took his eyes off them, working in their direction with the desperation of a swimmer whose strength was failing. They were moving away from him all the time, beginning to hasten, the woman with a handkerchief held to cover her head. Brennan brushed past a couple of bemedalled attachés, jacket flapping, unshaven, certain that only moments separated him from security intervention.

"Cooper."

For an appalled instant he believed that he was mistaken after all. They were only yards apart, yet even as his quarry turned the doubt hovered.

"Cooper?"

"Why, hallo," Cooper began, pivoting affably. "Damn shame the way—" It *was* Cooper, and even before the words died his trained smile was being erased by an expression of sheer incredulity. "Brennan!"

The woman in blue called: "Charles—"

"Just a moment, darling." Cooper stepped nearer, as if to hide Brennan from sight, and in a voice that shook he said: "My God, man, what are you doing here?"

CHAPTER FOURTEEN

In the distance the edge of the storm crumbled softly. They were being jostled as people flocked towards the marquee entrance.

"I've got to talk with you."

"But—"

"It's urgent."

Cooper's stunned alarm had the look of permanence. "I thought you were—"

"Charles," the woman called again over intervening heads, "I'm going in."

Cooper's eyes darted from side to side and Brennan misjudged him, fearing weakness; disownment, even. With desperation he said: "I'm in a jam . . . It's bad."

Incredibly, Cooper proceeded to greet somebody with a smile and a nod. Then to Brennan, louder than necessary and in an entirely different tone, he remarked: "When was this? During the last half-hour . . . Oh, very well," and Brennan found himself being steered against the tide. The band had given up and was sprinting for shelter. The rain was slanting down in rods. They shouldered clear of everyone, making for some trees, not stopping.

"What's happened? Give me something to go on."

"I need a doctor. Not for me—for someone else."

"I don't understand. Just how did you get in here?"

"By car."

"Dressed like that?"

He seemed so pained that Brennan misjudged him again. "I've got a wounded man on my hands, Cooper, and unless—"

"Wounded? Who?"

"Someone called Lloyd. He's been shot."

"My God," Cooper said. They had reached the trees. "Where is he?"

"In the car."

"Here? . . . My God," Cooper repeated, "you actually brought him *here*?"

"I couldn't take him to a hospital or to someone I didn't know. And he might be dead by eleven. He's losing blood all the time." Brennan was beginning to realise that he must be talking in riddles. "It's a long story. In a nutshell, I'm on the run. We both are. . . . There's a boat waiting to lift us off at eleven."

Cooper ignored all this. "Who shot him? Police?"

"Soldiers."

"Where?"

"Outside the morgue."

"The *morgue?*" Again Cooper sounded dumbfounded.

"We'd gone there to get some photographs, and—" Brennan gave up. "Does it matter? I'll explain later. It's too involved. But it's vital to get him to someone who won't turn him in, and you're the only one who can do it."

The clamour of a thousand voices rose from the horseshoe of yellow, lantern-like marquees. A few patrol guards had gathered for protection against a clump of near-by laurels.

"He's sunk unless you help," Brennan persisted.

Cooper said quietly: "Where's the car now?"

"I ran it in close to some glass-houses. Over there—off to the side."

"Tucked away?"

"Yes."

"Come on, then—but not too fast. Our friends are already curious and you can hardly blame 'em."

They walked circuitously—towards the nearest marquee, then between it and the next, then round the back until they were clear of the lights, after which they turned and hurried across the strip of grass that joined rear and front lawns. The party hum receded. Only then did Cooper speak again.

'It beats me how you got past the gates in the first place."

"Lloyd had an invitation."

"You, I said."

"I had a taxi-man's cap."

Cooper snorted with amazement. "Now where? You lead."

They moved between the driveway and the outer wall, floundering in the darkness. There were two distinct sounds—the clip of rain through leaves and the faint effervescent hiss of parched ground sopping up the wet. Presently Brennan reached the path that served the greenhouses. The car was still there and he felt a prickle of relief, one fear removed. He hurried on ahead of Cooper and unlocked the doors; clicked on the roof-light. Lloyd was arched between seat and floor and for half a moment Brennan thought he must be dead. But he groaned as Brennan shifted him, the ashen face contorting.

"How is he?" Cooper asked, peering from outside.

"Not good." Blood seemed to be everywhere. "I wasn't even able to bandage him properly. It's through the right shoulder, fairly low."

"How long ago did it happen?"

"Around eight." With a feeling of exhaustion Brennan tossed hair from his eyes. He looked at Cooper through the car. "D'you know of someone?"

"I think so. Though whether he'll be at home's another matter." The sky grumbled as Cooper swivelled his long legs into the car. His white tie drooped, but he was still sartorially elegant, decoration miniatures and all. "And first we've got to get ourselves out of here. . . . My God," he said reflectively, "you took a risk."

Brennan spread the raincoat completely over Lloyd and pulled on the peaked cap. "You do the talking, will you?"

"If there's any to be done." Cooper flicked his fingers. "Come on, let's see how we go. Traffic-scheme's one way, so you'll have to run the gauntlet."

Brennan nosed into the driveway and swung towards the Palace. The staircase and the entrance terrace were still flooded with lights, but deserted. It was impossibly late for anyone to be arriving and it began to look as though they would be allowed by without interference, but at the last moment a Palace guard left the protection of a wall and waved Brennan to a halt.

Cooper wound the window down. "It's all right, *guardia*. I'm on my way out."

"Señor?"

"I'm leaving . . . British Embassy."

Nonplussed, the guard came round to his side, the rain making havoc of his helmet-plumes. "Leaving, señor? But how can that be? The departure-point for guests is on the other—"

"I know. There's been a stupid mistake, but everything's in order now. No reflection on you. The mistake was mine, entirely mine. Good night, *guardia*."

His aplomb was immense. The guard nodded uncertainly and stood back, producing what passed for a salute. Brennan drew away and followed the temporary signs that serpentined them round to a side exit gate. There was another guard here, a few wretched policemen huddled under capes, but no danger. Seconds later the car was pointing down the long, glistening Avenida del Conquistador and Brennan began to shake as if every muscle in his body had taken on separate existence.

"Thanks, Cooper," he managed. He'd misjudged him all right.

"My dear fellow, that's what I'm here for—after a fashion." Cooper made an attempt to straighten his tie. "It makes a change from bailing-out bellicose seamen, I'll say that."

"Where do we go?"

"Steady as you are for the moment. . . . Cigarette? You look as though you need one. I certainly do." As he lit Brennan's, he asked "What was that about photographs?"

"I told you—it's a long story." Brennan blinked away sweat. He felt sick. "Lloyd's a journalist."

"Suppose you just tell me what you and he have been up to?"

"We broke into the morgue to get pictures of some of the people who were killed in that plane crash in Los Colmillos the other day." His voice was quite flat. "I dare say it sounds a mad thing to have done, but there were reasons—good reasons, but it'll take a month of Sundays to explain. I happened to be in the Colmillos when the plane came down, and—"

"Left, here," Cooper said. "And forget the explanations. Did you get the pictures?"

"Both times."

"Tonight?"

"Yes."

"Where are they?"

"The camera's somewhere in the back."

"First right." Cooper smoothed his hair with both hands—a gesture that might have conveyed excitement if Brennan's wits had been receptive enough. "Now take it easy. If anyone can patch Lloyd up it'll be Tim Hamilton, and if Tim isn't in I've another string to my bow. I'll get you both to Espada Point all right, don't worry."

Brennan glanced at him, startled. "When did I say anything about Espada Point?"

"You didn't." Cooper grinned. "You didn't have to. You see, you'll be using my motor-yacht. Frank Merchant asked permission to steal it off me only this morning." Then, without a pause: "Here, on the left—the archway . . . That's the one."

It was an angular house in a small, walled garden. A glimmer of light showed through the jalousies as they crunched under the porch and Cooper said "Might be just the servants, so keep your fingers crossed. Better stay where you are for the moment."

He heaved himself out and rang the bell. A long wait had to be endured before anyone answered, and Brennan watched anxiously, thoughts churning. When the door at last was opened it was by a thick-set, sandy-haired man in shirt-sleeves with whom Cooper spent a minute or two's intense, inaudible conversation. Then he turned, giving the thumbs-up sign, and came back to the car.

"Couldn't be better. Servants' night off and Tim's already forgotten we ever called. Now . . . shall I take his legs?"

Lloyd was considerably heavier than he looked. With difficulty they got him slung between them and carried him into the house. Once inside, Hamilton directed them into a clinically-bare room where they lowered Lloyd carefully on to a high couch. There was also a desk in the room, a couple of chairs, some cabinets, a trolley—not much else. Lloyd didn't make a sound. Now his face showed the years: every line—every sag.

Cooper said: "Not only is Tim a bachelor but he's about the only person in the British community who didn't apply to go to the ball."

"Once was enough," Hamilton retorted. He was a Scot, brusque and businesslike. "Cooper tells me your friend was shot around eight o'clock, is that right?"

Brennan nodded. "About then, yes."

"Since when he's been unconscious?"

"Except for a minute or two."

Hamilton grunted and bent across the couch. After a little while he muttered "If you want to talk somewhere there's whisky in the living-room."

"Is he going to be okay?"

"Give me a chance to look at him, will you?"

"He's got a journey to make," Cooper said.

"So you told me, but I'm a doctor not a prophet. Go and drink my whisky, for Pete's sake. I've work to do."

They closed the door on him and crossed the hall. In the living-room Brennan subsided immediately into an armchair. He felt so worn out that he couldn't think properly.

"*Your* boat?" he queried, as if Cooper had that second sprung his surprise. "Was that some kind of joke?"

"Certainly not. . . . Here, find a home for this."

Brennan took the tumbler. Wearily, he said: "What else don't I know?"

Cooper shrugged. "As you said yourself, it's a long story. Anyway, I've got some questions of my own. I think the biggest shock I've ever had was finding you at my elbow in the lion's den tonight." He drank, tossing back his head. "D'you remember what you called yourself when we last met?"

"Not exactly."

"A perpetual tourist."

"Did I?"

"Tourists don't normally go breaking into public morgues or gate-crashing Presidential parties, even at the best of times. What changed you? You've come a long way from humming-birds."

"I haven't changed." Brennan moved his hands. "I . . . I just got caught up in things."

"To the extent of risking your neck when you needn't have?"

"The morgue was Lloyd's idea."

"But you went along."

"I know how to use a camera, that's why."

"No other reason?"

"Does it matter?"

"I'm curious. For a couple of days one of the world's small cold wars has been in progress, and here you are—the professed disdainer, as it were—with the rope that López might hang from neatly in your pocket." Cooper's pale blue eyes fixed on him quizzically. "Wasn't that at any time in your mind?"

"Not really."

"Extraordinary." He said it twice, dragging the word out.

"How long have *you* been aware of what was in the wind?"

"Frank Merchant rang me on Friday to say that it looked as if you might have stumbled on to something and would I keep an eye on you."

Brennan had lost track of days. He had survived so much. "Was that before I called at the Embassy?"

"Oh yes. I'm afraid I deceived you that morning—made out I didn't know who you were."

"I don't recall being chaperoned. Followed, yes. But—"

"My dear fellow," Cooper smiled, "you pitched my man into the swimming-pool."

Brennan shook his head in disbelief.

"Listen," Cooper said. "The Americans have never much cared for López. At most it's been a case of the devil they knew. And in recent months he's been suspected of looking enviously at Castro. Also of having made a few secret overtures to Moscow. There was no proof, of course—nothing positive that might pin him down until you went into the Oasis Club on Friday and told Merchant what had happened near Pozoblanco. Frank cocked his ear at that, as well he might. In our business these are the trickles that sometimes eventually split rocks." He lifted a decanter. "More?"

"Not for me."

"Unfortunately it wasn't until Saturday morning that Frank heard about the pictures you'd taken. Miss Stacey apparently mentioned them, but it was too late. Vega had López's gun in his back long before then: obviously, you were followed to his place the previous evening. Obviously, too, López was hiding something of the utmost consequence."

Brennan shifted his position in the chair. "Wouldn't it have been more realistic if someone had told me what was going on? You, for instance." He glared, raw-eyed, capable of anger even now. "I should have thought—"

"There's such a thing as secrecy."

"Oh, sure. Little children should be seen but not heard."

"Good God, Brennan, one can't automatically confide in a member of the public every time he's unwittingly involved himself in something. It depends on the circumstances. In this case there was always the chance that López was going to haul you in—you were the only fly in his ointment—and the Americans were desperately keen not to have him know they suspected anything. The best we could do was to try and keep a watch on you so that if you were removed *á la* Vega we'd be aware of it. But then you went off on the warpath on your own. We lost you. Miss Stacey did her best, but you weren't having any."

"You'll tell me next that she was acting under orders as well."

"I couldn't say. The Americans don't even tell *us* everything."

He smiled again, ruefully, then put his glass down. "You know, I'd feel happier if that camera of yours weren't out in the car."

"It's Lloyd's," Brennan said.

"All the same I'll fetch it in." On the way across the hall he evidently looked in on Hamilton because there were some murmured exchanges. When he returned with the Yashica he said: "Tim's interim report's encouraging. And the wind's dropping, even if the rain's heavier than ever." His expression changed as he studied the camera. "It's damaged, did you know?"

"I had to chuck it over some railings, but the film won't be harmed."

"Merchant's going to want it—I suppose you realise that?"

"It isn't mine to give. Legally it might even be the property of the *Sunday Herald*."

"Lloyd wouldn't say no. He couldn't anyway—not with what's at stake. The Americans have an idea who was on that plane. Only the proof's lacking."

"Let's wait and ask him, shall we?" Brennan closed his eyes. It wasn't a time for splitting hairs, but his mind was filled with a dozen memories of Lloyd and what his day of obligation had cost him in nerve and pain.

"After all," Cooper said, "he's been hunting the same fox."

"Not for the same reasons."

"Not exactly, of course. The story's an end in itself for these fellows. And I must say I take off my hat—"

"It wasn't even because of the story."

"I don't think I understand."

"Nor did I, but I do now." Brennan let it go at that; rubbed his face. One whisky, and he felt a little drunk. He had misjudged everyone at one time or another—even, it appeared, Frank Merchant. First Merchant, then Vega, then Alison . . . Years seemed to have passed in his brain since he read her note. *Dearest Harry*. A longing for her throbbed through his exhaustion and he said "About Miss Stacey—"

"Yes?"

"Is there a chance of my contacting her before we leave?"

"Every chance, I should have thought."

"Will she be at Espada Point?"

174

"If she isn't the *Black Orchid*'s going to be without a driver."
Cooper seemed to find genuine pleasure in watching Brennan's
astonishment. "My dear fellow, didn't I tell you? . . . Miss
Stacey's taking you and Lloyd across."

When Hamilton eventually joined them Brennan could
scarcely wait for him to enter the room. "Well?"

"He'll be fine—notwithstanding the way the poor devil's been
manhandled." He eyed them both. "As far as I can tell it missed
the lung, missed the clavicle, nicked the shoulder-blade on the
way in and made a mess of the deltoid muscle—I'll spare you
the details since they clearly don't mean a thing. Just let's say
he's been lucky. Very, very lucky." He rolled down his sleeves
and poured himself a whisky.

Cooper said : "Can we have a word with him?"

"In the morning."

"Not before?"

"I've put him under, Charles. Be sensible."

"He can travel, though?"

"I gather he has to, so what can I say?" He drank. "Yes, he
can travel. And to ease my conscience I've written a note to
whoever it may concern. Here"—he handed it to Brennan—
"you're dressed for the part so I presume you're going along."

"Thanks." For the first time in days Brennan found the
ability to shape a smile.

Cooper glanced at his watch. "Look, Tim," he said, "we'll
be off your doorstep in a matter of minutes, but first I want to
use your phone. All right?"

"Go ahead."

"I had to leave the Palace without Mary knowing and I'm
afraid she's still there. It's hardly the best place for her the way
things are."

Hamilton stroked his nose. "I suppose it would be wiser if I
didn't ask what way that is?"

"Much wiser."

"That's what I thought." He grimaced cheerfully.

Cooper went to the telephone and requested a number. While
he waited to be connected he covered the mouthpiece.

"The Embassy," he explained gently. Then "Mr. Lamb, please . . . Lamb? Cooper . . . Look, two things. First I want a car sent to the Palace immediately to pick up my wife. Get Sergeant Mace to do it. He'll have to have her paged or whatever the form is . . . No, I'm not there and I left her rather in the lurch. Yes, yes. Mace . . ." Behind the throttled voice and languid manner he was quick-witted and as firm as iron: Brennan could see it now. "Second, I want the Rover for myself as soon as possible. And not at the usual place—get that? . . . *Not* the usual one, no . . . Ten minutes? Good."

Cooper rang off. "I've been spoiled, you know. Without some CD armour I feel almost naked—tonight especially. We aren't out of the wood yet."

"What about the car you came in?" This was Hamilton.

"We're taking it, don't worry. What's more, we're taking it right now. Confucius say 'Swinging chain mean warm seat', remember, and if they're casting their net as—"

"They?" Hamilton queried.

"Read all about it, Tim. Forget you ever saw us."

Cooper led them across the hall to the room where Lloyd was lying. His right arm was slung; the shoulder elaborately bandaged. His breathing was slow and deep and his sponged face looked more relaxed than Brennan had ever seen it. Cooper went out and switched off the porch light. When he returned, he and Hamilton carried Lloyd to the car, after which Hamilton doubled back for a couple of cushions which he slid under Lloyd's head.

"A boat, is it?" he asked, curiosity surfacing.

"Yes." The rain was drumming down. Brennan had the camera.

"I don't envy him. Or you," he said to Brennan. "But he's up to it. Looks worse than he is, but a couple of days and he won't know himself."

"Thanks a lot, Tim," Cooper said. "And don't forget your fee."

"You were never here. That's my story and I'm sticking to it." Hamilton made a succession of shooing motions. "*Bon voyage* and good luck."

Brennan followed Cooper's directions and turned left along the street.

"Is this thing yours?"

"Lloyd was renting it." They made a hundred yards or so. "Where's '*not* the usual place'?"

"Business quarter. But the longest mile's the last."

The streets were like glass under the sodium-lamps. Brennan drove carefully, blind but for the twin arcs of the wipers, the tyres running with a continuous squelch. Lloyd was covered over with the raincoat. Twice they saw police, and an army wagon once prowled ominously across their path. SI LÓPEZ SI! a slogan read, and Cooper growled: "Yes, what?" They changed course perhaps half a dozen times until they reached the business quarter, deserted on a Sunday night anyway, rain or no rain. The new office blocks towered into the streaming darkness, interspersed by building-sites marked for sale. Cooper suddenly said: "Over there," and Brennan found himself swinging into a lane between vacant weed-covered lots. Parked just off to the side was the Embassy Rover and he drew in close by, bumping over the corduroy grain of soggy earth. "Cut your lights," Cooper urged.

The man at the wheel of the Rover emerged smartly and clicked his heels as if he were in uniform. "Good evening, sir. Mr. Lamb said I was to expect you."

"Hallo, Jenkins." Cooper struggled out, stooping against the downpour. Brennan followed suit. It was almost impossible to see.

"Mr Lamb didn't say what it was in aid of, Mr. Cooper."

"Open up, will you? There's someone here we have to transfer. And be careful with him. He's wounded."

"Yes, sir." Jenkins showed no surprise. Together they moved Lloyd on to the back seat of the Rover, then squeezed themselves into the front. The doors thudded. "What about the other car, sir?"

"Leave it." Cooper said, mopping his hair with a handkerchief. "Short cut through to Conquistador, then make for Espada Point."

"Beyond Monterrey?"

"That's it. And keep an eye out behind. If you think anyone's on your tail, let me know. That's about the only risk now. There's no hurry, so for God's sake take it easy."

They lurched back to the lane and drew smoothly away. "Is the gentleman badly hurt, sir?"

Cooper rocked one finger-splayed hand.

Jenkins dog-legged clear of the business quarter, heading towards the heart of the old city through a jungle of tight, neon-blurred streets. Bars, cafés, pin-table saloons. PARKER PENS . . . TRY AN EYE-OPENER . . . EAT AT THE GOLDEN SPURS . . . PEPSI-COLA . . . Normality pressed in from all sides, but Brennan wasn't on terms with it yet and when the Rover splashed level with a row of tatty rooming-houses where a squad of police was knocking people up he knew tension again.

"Lot of activity tonight," Jenkins remarked meaningly. "Noticed it on my way to meet you."

Cooper nodded. "He keeps trying, I'll say that for him."

"Sir?"

"Forget it, Jenkins. Anything behind?"

"No."

The Avenida del Conquistador came and went; then the Casino. Dimly, Brennan realised that he was seeing them for the last time, but he was too spent to care one way or the other. Even when they turned near Vega's and he glimpsed the shuttered windows he felt nothing. Too much had happened. Reaction was setting in, tugging him down, and only the thought of Alison kept him from yielding to it. It was almost ten forty as they went by the tram terminus. From there on La Paz started its gradual disintegration and the sense of release grew as he smelt the hot, wet land. Hope strengthened in him; thankfulness. But he needed time.

"How d'you feel?" Cooper asked. "Pole-axed?"

"Just about."

The rain fell like gold through the beam of the headlights. Starkly transfigured trees blurred and vanished into the rushing dark. They passed the track which led off to the cock-fight arena. The road swung coastwards in the direction of Monterrey and brought them near the beaches, one journey almost done, another about to begin. Monterrey didn't last—a deserted *plaza*, haphazard clusters of lights, a group of youths sheltering by the church—and Cooper warned: "You'll have to turn off before long."

"Yes, sir. I know, sir." Jenkins had never left the parade-ground.

Soon there was a fork, left to Pozoblanco, right to nowhere in particular, as uncertain as the future itself. They quit the metalled surface and bore right, reducing speed.

"Nothing behind, sir."

Now, through the smeared glass, there were cactus hedges and divi-divis and broken-down plantations. The road deteriorated as it wandered, becoming swampy. After they had covered a couple of miles from the fork Cooper began to peer ahead. Once there was a brief view of waves thudding on black volcanic sand. Presently the road made up its mind and started on a symmetrical sweep that brought them round the rim of a small, wooded bay. Presently again, without apparent reason, Cooper ordered Jenkins to stop.

"This'll do." To Brennan he said: "Stay here. Won't be longer than I can help."

He left the car and squelched away, refusing the offer of Jenkins's coat. There was fantasy in the headlight glimpse of his sodden tails and dangling miniatures. Jenkins clucked his tongue ruefully. "Mrs. Cooper *will* be pleased . . . Cigarette, sir?"

"Thanks."

Lloyd was breathing deeply and his pulse was slow but strong. They waited for several minutes. Brennan couldn't make out where they were: the rain and the dark and the surrounding trees were all of a piece. He sat with the camera on his lap. Jenkins's only remark was: "To think back home they say Manchester's wet. It's a laugh, that is. A real laugh." The rest of the time he whistled tunelessly, tapping his fingers on the wheel. He might have been in a lay-by. Eventually there was movement over to their right and they saw Cooper returning. Merchant was with him, hatted, rain-proofed; wearing gumboots. Jenkins jumped out and held the door for them.

"God, Brennan, am I glad to see you."

"Hallo, Merchant," Brennan said.

It was hard at that moment to remember the old antagonism. The four of them crowded in on the bench-seat, Merchant craning round to look at Lloyd.

"The so-and-so." The drawl was admiring. "He never breathed a word about what he had in mind. Not a word . . And as for you"—he grinned at Brennan—"I gather you made the Palace after all."

"Where's Alison?"

Merchant nodded, vaguely indicating the direction from which he had appeared. "Everything's set for go. . . . But first I want to hear about those pictures Charles tells me you and Lloyd got tonight. Are you quite sure they're of the same man?"

"Sure."

"The one who was in that tree?"

"Positive."

"Did Lloyd identify him?"

"I don't believe so, but we didn't exactly have time for a cosy chat."

"Charles says you feel Lloyd ought to be consulted before you part with them."

"They're his property."

"Look, Brennan, so much depends on what's on that film that I can't even begin to tell you. But if we can confront López with proof that he's been dabbling with a Communist infiltration of the Western hemisphere—"

"You've no alternative," Cooper put in.

"We can't wait for Lloyd. I want them tonight. Now in fact."

"I'm not quibbling," Brennan said. "But Lloyd would do a deal with you and so shall I."

Wearily he gazed from one to the other. You got them, chum, he thought. But getting them was the thing—for you it was. You know that? and so do I.

"What deal?" Merchant frowned.

"They're his. Exclusively. The story, too."

"I can hardly put it in writing."

"Your word will do."

"All I want is some prints. The negatives will be in to-morrow's diplomatic bag."

"Plus any information he deserves to have."

"I'll give him what's possible."

"I'll hold you to that, so help me."

Brennan looked at them again, then began to wind the film to an end.

"No switches," Merchant joked, as if disturbed by the intensity of his stare. "Not again."

"And no making out I botched them up."

He opened the Yashica and handed the spool to Merchant. A prolonged shiver moved through him as he parted with it. He wanted to say something more about Lloyd and the high wire he'd forced himself to walk something about the story that no one would ever write, not even in the *Sunday Herald*. But he let the thought go.

Merchant said "Thanks, Brennan."

"Don't thank me. None of it was my idea."

"You beat us all at our own game."

Brennan smiled, strained, the shiver ending. "How about someone showing me how the hell we get ourselves off this blasted island?"

They eased Lloyd out of the car, Jenkins and Cooper and Merchant between them. Brennan draped the raincoat over him and they stumbled into the trees. Cooper mentioned something about the *Black Orchid*, her safety, her capabilities; and Merchant said that Kingston had been warned to expect them. But Brennan was listening for the sea; looking for it through the hiss of the rain. The ground sloped gently down. Finally, they emerged on to a long, slippery mossy ledge that hooked round to form a small basin.

Cooper grunted: "There she is," and with a lift of his heart Brennan saw Alison standing in the cockpit of the boat waiting for them.

CHAPTER FIFTEEN

THE rain kept on, but the wind that brought it had died. Now and again, along the western horizon, lightning flapped and the night growled a harmless diapason. The *Black Orchid* plunged through a quartering sea on a northward course, nose digging deep. Spray came bulleting off the wave-tops in stinging cascades, rattling like fusillades of shot against the ventilators and cabin-top. Santa Marta had vanished on their starboard beam but Brennan still hadn't gone below except to make a check that Lloyd was securely strapped in his bunk.

"Go on, Harry. Get some sleep."

"Soon."

"I'm serious. You need it. You look awful."

"There's all night yet." He wedged himself more firmly into a corner of the wheelhouse, weary beyond words yet happy in a way he had never been. "I didn't know you were a seaman, too."

"There's a lot you don't know." She stood at the wheel with a plastic coat over her jeans and sweatshirt, legs braced, hair wet and loose. The light from the compass-bowl softly illuminated her face.

"Tell me."

"Some other time."

Water crashed under the bow and the *Black Orchid* shook. He watched Alison with drooping eyes, marvelling at her competence, discovering once again how much he needed her.

"Were you in it from the beginning?"

" 'In it'?"

"Everyone else seems to have been."

"I didn't know a thing," she said, "until Frank asked me to try and put a curb on you."

"That was his idea?"

She nodded. "He said you were meddling with something you didn't understand, and that the more you got to know the more dangerous it could be. I've never hated doing anything so much in my whole life."

"And what about now? Was this his idea, too?"

"No."

"Whose, then?"

"Mine." A veil of spindrift scudded over. "Don't pick bones, Harry. Post-mortems are for the dead."

"No bones. But I wanted to hear you say it."

She was as gentle with him as with a child. "Well, I've said it, so go below and get some rest."

"Why should you be the loser?"

"I won't be."

"Your job, though." He moved his hands, flayed muscles already aching from trying to keep his balance. "The whole Oasis set-up. You liked it there. . . . I feel as guilty as hell."

"Nonsense."

"What are you going to do?"

"I'll tell you another day."

"Now."

"No," she said. "Not now. You're too tired."

In a voice cracked with fatigue he said: "Barring Lloyd, you're the most determined person I've ever met."

"And you're the most stubborn—bar none." She smiled. "Go on, Harry. Go away. Let me concentrate. I've another eight or nine hours of this."

"Can't I help?"

"I'll shout if I need you."

He lurched from his corner, defeated by the struggle to remain awake, stamina at an end. As he passed Alison he kissed her hard on the mouth and she clung to him briefly. "Harry," she said, "Harry, I've been so frightened." Then a heeling movement of the boat parted them and Brennan staggered out of the wheelhouse and climbed down to the tiny cabin where Lloyd slept his drugged sleep. He flung himself on to the other bunk and plummeted into unconsciousness with the salt taste of her wet lips still fresh upon his.

It seemed as if no time at all had passed when he opened his eyes and stared up at the deckhead. His mind fastened on to the reassuring thump-thump of the engine: then, as the wakening jigsaw pieced together, he turned and looked across the cabin. Lloyd had scarcely shifted. Brennan swung stiffly to his feet and went over to him; studied the slightly flushed face. It was strange to think that, not all that time ago, he had borne him malice. Ouside, it was still dark but the rain had ceased and the sea was no longer broken and confused. He heaved himself up the ladder and joined Alison, aching in every limb.

"D'you call that a rest?"

"What time is it?" He fondled her neck as if she already belonged to him.

"Half-five."

"I could tackle something unskilled like making coffee. What d'you say?"

"Would you, Harry?" She yawned.

"Sure."

"How's the patient?"

"Seems all right. But the sooner he's in proper hands the happier I'll be. How much longer, d'you think?"

"A couple of hours with luck."

The malignant cloud-cover had dispersed. Now there were stars in the sky. He went down to the galley and started the coffee on the stove. Presently, above the unending crunch of cloven water he thought he heard a sound from the cabin. Hurrying there, he found that Lloyd had twisted round in the bunk. As he straightened him Lloyd muttered thickly: "The camera, chum. Where's the camera?"—a slowly surfacing corner of his brain still presumably believing himself in the car; still living the nightmare. Brennan covered him and returned to the stove, moved, Merchant's promise hanging between him and the feeling of having committed an act of betrayal.

When he reappeared through the hatchway an opal smear along the eastern rim was beginning to separate the elements. He made his way awkwardly to the wheelhouse, coffee slopping from the pot both while he carried it and while he poured two steaming cups. They sipped it together. Dawn took hold, sapphire and pink, and the stars switched off in groups. The *Black*

Orchid ploughed on, trailing a marble wash: Alison doused the riding lights. Moist and warm, a land breeze found them, seemingly meant for them alone, and the first gulls showed up, wheeling like scraps of paper. An hour passed, an hour during which they scarcely spoke, sharing weariness now, dull eyes reflecting the bright water. A pair of dolphins came to nose playfully ahead of the bow wave like polished steel torpedoes, occasionally scorning the *Black Orchid*'s steady ten knots with displays of vast speed. And eventually Jamaica disclosed itself, no more than a bruise along the skyline to begin with, then with increasing beauty.

Alison spun the wheel, heading north-east. For some twenty minutes they ran against the landward nudge of the swell along a coast of salt-white beaches backed by a tumult of green and blue hills until the *Black Orchid* was on course again and the mouth of Kingston harbour was opening up, waiting to receive them.

There were no difficulties. A police-launch escorted them in and they were chaperoned through Immigration. An ambulance was already on the jetty for Lloyd: it bore him away with the letter Hamilton had given Brennan. A young, soft-spoken Jamaican, who introduced himself but seemed to assume they knew in what official capacity he was acting, drove them in his car to a hotel. Rooms had been booked and there was even a note at the desk for Brennan asking him to present himself at the office of the High Commissioner as early as it was convenient "for any assistance you may require". Cooper and Merchant between them had clearly wasted neither effort nor time.

"When shall I see you, Harry?" Alison asked as the elevator took them to their floor.

"You say."

"Five-ish?"

"Fine." It was nine thirty now. He kissed her forehead. "I'll look like a pauper, mind."

"What about me?"

"You'll still be marvellous."

He ran a bath; soaked himself. Afterwards he telephoned the hospital where Lloyd had been taken and asked to be put through to the sister-in-charge. Everything had moved so quickly on their arrival that he hadn't had his wits about him. Lloyd was stirring, apparently. "Will you tell him," he said, "that Mr. Brennan says he's not to worry about the photographs. . . . The photographs, yes. I'll look in later—tell him that, too, please. It's most important." Afterwards he telephoned cables to Benedict at *Four Seasons* and to *InterconTel*. The future was on its way, but the past wasn't done with. Ravenously, he ate the breakfast sent up to him, then curled on the bed and stared at the immaculate ceiling, his tired mind jammed with a dozen memories of fear and wonder.

He couldn't believe Merchant would go back on his word, but the doubt nagged and he took it under through the trapdoor which suddenly opened for him.

He had asked for a call at half past three. When it came he got up at once and dressed, then went down to the desk and exchanged the few SM dollars still in his possession. They didn't amount to much; enough for a shave and a taxi or two. He had the shave in the barber's-shop below, after which he braved the implacable dazzle of Kingston's mid-afternoon.

The hospital wasn't far. He paid the taxi off and mounted the wide steps into the cool of the entrance lobby.

"Mr. Lloyd?" a man queried from behind glass. "Matthew Lloyd?"

Brennan nodded; followed the directions. On the second landing a nurse with a double-octave smile and a gliding walk led him along a glistening corridor. Yes, Mr. Lloyd was fine. Just fine. But he wasn't to be over-taxed. Ten minutes would be ample. . . . She pushed a door open and stood back to allow Brennan through.

"Chum."

Brennan moved swiftly to the bed; gripped the extended hand. "How is it?"

"Could be worse. But I'm losing no opportunity to complain."

"You got my message?"

"I did indeed." Lloyd's voice was low. His eyes had a feverish look and his lips were dry. He patted the bed. "Squat," he said. "Someone told me you were roughing it in a hotel."

"That's right." Brennan smiled uneasily. "There's no justice."

"Someone also told me this is Kingston."

"Right again."

"The rest, to coin a phrase, is a blank. The last thing I remember was being near *The Conch Shell* in López-land. What happened?"

Brennan hesitated. Primarily, he had come to explain about the photographs; but now that he was there he jibbed at mentioning them. Lloyd was already savouring triumph. The feeble jauntiness had its roots in the certainty of achievement and Brennan thought it best to stall.

"Hell, chum," Lloyd prompted. "I've got a story to file—remember?"

"It's a bit involved."

"Well, I'm all ears. A to Z, though. I've a simple mind at the best of times."

He listened intently. Once he whistled. Once his eyes narrowed. Finally he chuckled. "I've got to hand it to you. God, I have."

"Incidentally," Brennan said, "I bought the coat and cap mostly with your money. In fact I've just had a shave on the strength of what was left."

"Good for you. My life's worth forty or fifty pesos any time." For a moment he showed emotion and his free hand fisted against Brennan's thigh. "I'll get around to thanking you properly one of these days."

"Balls."

There was a slight pause. Then, with a sigh, Lloyd said: "Well, I nearly made it. As near as dammit, eh?"

"You made it all the way."

"You're very kind, chum." He rolled his head. "But it's not true—as you and I know. I couldn't have gone near the place alone. I needed the pictures, yes—but there was more to it than that. It's got *too* hard . . . Too hard," he repeated. "I kid you not. Glory boy's run his course."

"You came out a winner, though."

"Sure, sure. Matthew Lloyd was actually there for once." He licked his lips. Then, brightening, he gestured toward the bedside-table. "The envelope, chum. D'you mind?" It was a large, plain manilla with heavy, fractured seals. Brennan leaned across and offered it to him, but he waved it away. "You do it. I'm as clumsy as Nelson."

Brennan slid the contents on to the quilt. There were three smaller envelopes. Even as he picked up the first he could feel that it contained photographs, half-plates at a guess, but the surprise didn't really hit him until he took them out and found himself confronted by the flash-lit face of the man in the morgue drawer.

"When did you get these?"

"Couple of hours ago."

"From?"

"Someone who merely said they were with the compliments of a Mr. Merchant. He'd gone before the penny dropped."

"What's in the others?"

"See for yourself. Wasn't that what your message meant?"

"It's what I hoped it would mean."

"Ah."

There were negatives in the second envelope. Brennan glanced at them briefly, then opened the third. Inside was a note, folded across the middle.

Dear Mr Lloyd:

Harry Brennan will by now have explained the circumstances and probably bitten his nails down to the quick into the bargain.

Photographs—negatives and prints herewith—are of one Vladimir Yaronsky, 52, Russian economic counsellor, known to have been active two years ago in Cuba. Make of it what you will subject to normal clearance procedures. The lid will be off within 24 hours. Look forward to receiving a copy of Sunday's Herald, *by which time sincerely trust that you are well on the road to recovery.*

Yours,
Frank Merchant.

As Brennan raised his eyes, Lloyd said: "What else could you have done? . . . Anyhow, it's over. All's well that ends well, and it might just make a line in the history books at that."

The dark nurse came in. "I'm sorry, Mr. Lloyd, but your friend has been with you plenty long enough."

"Rubbish."

Brennan rose. "I'll look in tomorrow. What can I do meanwhile?"

"Not a thing, thanks. I've cabled the *Herald* and asked for someone to fly out with a typewriter and a bunch of grapes." He grinned, very pale on the pillow, sweating thinly. "By the way, you haven't said a word about Miss Stacey. She couldn't have done what she did because of me, chum, so I reckon—"

"Please, Mr. Lloyd," the nurse cut in.

"Isn't she beautiful?" Lloyd said weakly. "Off you go, Brennan. Don't you know when you're in the way?"

Outside, the sun was as fierce as ever. Brennan went down the steps two at a time. It was a quarter to five and he wanted to be with Alison.

Also published in

CORONET BOOKS

ACT OF MERCY

by Francis Clifford

Tom Jordan finds himself immediately involved in a local revolution in South America when he discovers the deposed President unconscious in his garden—weak with fatigue and with a price on his head.

There were three choices open to him, surrender Camara, the ex-President, to the revolutionaries; turn him away or help him to escape to the frontier.

Haunted by the death rattle of the firing squads, Tom decides to run for the frontier with his wife Susan and Camara.

By the end of the day Tom and his wife are being hunted as much as the man they are trying to save and they have only just begun to taste the bitter fruits of courage and generosity in a world of callous brutality.

"A spare, gripping, Amblerish novel; fast-moving, full of action and quietly impressive throughout."

The Daily Telegraph

THE THIRD SIDE OF THE COIN
by Francis Clifford

Anyone might get a chance like this, but only a man whose life was in ruins was prepared to take it. In Anthony Pascoe, something had rotted, making him weak enough, crazy enough to yield to the temptation to cut loose and begin again.

The agonies of this man on the run who could hardly believe in his own bravado started at London Airport at eight minutes past three on a normal Saturday afternoon. They ended in a moment of agonising choice as the dust settled on an earth-quake-shattered town in southern Spain.

"Immensely gripping."

Daily Worker

"Accomplished."

The Scotsman

"Traumatic."

The Times Literary Supplement

BESTSELLING THRILLERS BY FRANCIS CLIFFORD

All these books are available at your bookshop or newsagent, or can be ordered direct from the publisher. Just tick the titles you want and fill in the form below.

....

CORONET BOOKS, Cash Sales Department, Kernick Industrial Estate, Penryn, Cornwall.

Please send cheque or postal order. No currency, and allow 7p per book (6p per book on orders of five copies and over) to cover the cost of postage and packing in U.K., 7p per copy overseas.

Name..

Address...

....